AFTER THE WAR

STORIES FROM THE NEXT REGIME

Edited by

WOLAND

Foreword by

ZERO HP LOVECRAFT

First published 2024 by Passage Publishing

For information, contact support@passage.press

Trade Paperback ISBN: 978-1-959403-04-3

Passage Publishing
www.passage.press

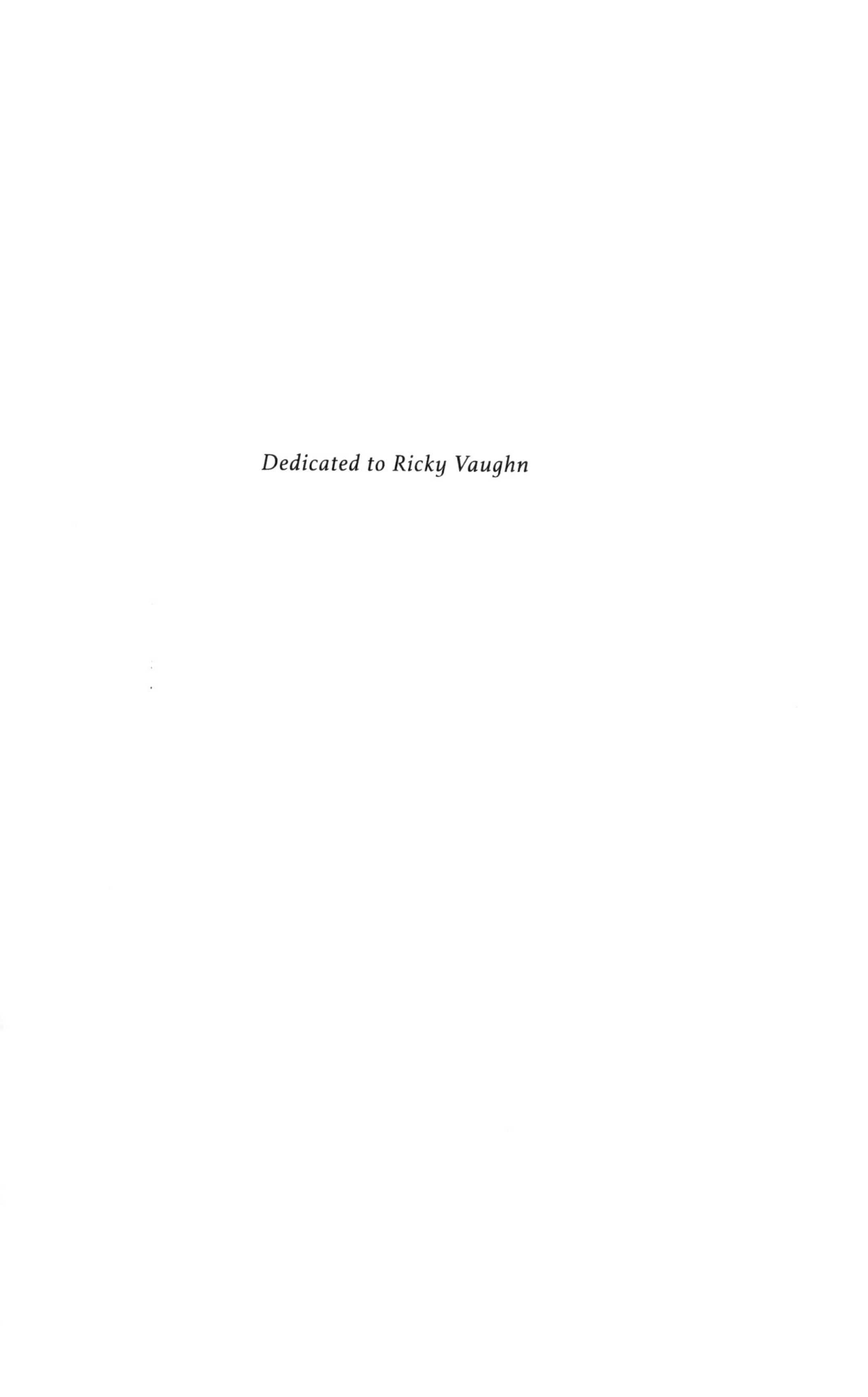

Dedicated to Ricky Vaughn

FOREWORD

ZERO HP LOVECRAFT

When I was asked to write the intro to this book, I was pleased to see that so many of my friends had made contributions. All of them are worthy, but being worthy is not a single act, it is a continuous process.

This is an anthology of flash fiction and as such, it would be unbecoming for me to write an introduction to it which is longer than any of the stories themselves. What decadence, what self-importance, how tasteless that would be! No, there's nothing at all to say about a story which is 500 words long, and to attempt such a commentary is surely an insult to the authors. Instead—and at the risk of being trite—I will offer you some meditations on the format.

A work of flash fiction is a special case of a joke, or maybe a joke is a special case of flash fiction: that is, a flash story has the structure of a joke, even more so than other short forms. The structure contains a setup and a punchline, and what makes it a joke is that the intention of the punchline is to make you laugh, whereas in flash fiction writ large, the punchline usually wants to invoke some other emotion: guilt, terror, remorse, surprise... occasionally even delight. Short stories and their kin aim for emotional impact, so they tend towards the macabre. In that sense, the flash fiction is a kind of anti-joke, a joke for the minions of hell, who, upon hearing it, take a perverse enjoyment in a painful emotion, though in fact many of the stories in this collection are hopeful.

In this age of emails and tweets and phone notifications, they tell us the novel is dead. Who is going to sit still long enough to read one? It seems contemporary movies and television are increasingly reduced to a series of rapid cuts designed to overstimulate the viewer in a frenzied bid to hold their attention. A novel is now a soundtrack that we listen to in the background as we scroll on our phones. Against this backdrop of narrative compression, a single flash fiction may begin to feel like the one-point-three million word, seven novel saga *In Search of Lost Time* by Marcel Proust.

Everyone has heard the idea that we die each morning when we sleep, only to be reborn when we awaken, but let me propose an even more radical version of this thought: each time our attention shifts from one context to another, each time we alight like a butterfly on each new bloom within the mind, there is a discontinuity in our consciousness, and a new iteration of the self is born. It may be that you are a new person each time you pass through a door, or glance up from a book or a phone, each time someone interrupts you in a day dream.

Well, a flash fiction story is short enough that you can conceivably read one story, not only in a single sitting, but in a single interval of consciousness, with no momentary discontinuity. If you really grit your teeth and muscle through it, you can read a whole two pages without even once switching contexts to check your social media feeds. It may take Herculean discipline, monumental effort, but such a feat may be, in this sense I have just described, the longest moment of your goldfish life.

They say the bit of folk trivia about a goldfish having a memory of three seconds is just that: a folk tale, but there's still something so poignant about this image. Trapped in a glass bowl, watched on all sides, an attention span of three seconds: that's me, that's you.

CONTENTS

1

DEAD WHITE ASTRONAUTS

V.N. EBERT

There's not much on the Moon but we're there. Geodesic domes on stilts driven in deep. The surface is so unstable and porous you have to build on it like building on a sea.

I was a pilot. I did hops between the bases. Flying in 0.166 G's is a strange thing. Essentially, you get talented enough at that, you can't fly on Earth anymore because your reflexes are off.

The Moon had been a libertarian thing and didn't really work out that way. Like most undertakings that go on long enough and take on enough scale to matter, there's an adventure that's mostly at the beginning when you weren't around and people who were heroic and lucky were. They're the ones who get written about, and then the bureaucracy sets in and everything slowly turns varying shades of grey.

I was living at the grey bureaucracy stage. The colonies had enough people on them that you could get discussion of whether we should be called "Moon-persons" or "Lunarians," even if "Moonies" and "Lunatics" were more popular in common usage than the leadership admitted, and the occasional story about the discrimination we faced when we went down to the Green Spot. I suppose being a grievance group shows you've made it, from one way of looking at things.

But I liked watching the Green Spot out over the Sea of Tranquility. We've always got it with us, thanks to the synchronous orbit. Could see the clouds. Can track typhoons and hurricanes making their way across the green-blue sphere. Things that are violent at close range but peaceful with enough distance—enough to enable a kind-of detached perspective.

I remember trying to tell something like that to a girl who was a recent arrival on one of the rockets from the Green Spot. We don't get so many arrivals, and when somebody new enters into what amounts to a closed community that person will attract attention.

She had an unsettled air about her, and at first we chalked some of that up to her needing to find her legs. That is, get adjusted to the gravity. New way of living.

But, she didn't acclimate well. Wanted to go organize, whatever that meant. She said she was part of an organization and a collective and was recruiting, and that meant going to the various bases. I ended up flying her and you end up knowing your regulars.

I was getting a dehydrated coffee in the terminal, and she was scheduled for that hop. She must've committed herself to trying to recruit me because she came straight up to me from the entrance area with a flier in her hand.

It had some designs on it I wasn't familiar with and a rainbow flag I remembered from down there. Been a while, but I remembered. There was some stuff about the imminent end of the world. That was all about the Green Spot and not us here. I guess she hadn't thought to get a different flier made for the new audience, because we didn't quite share her perspective, being as we were some distance away.

She gave her pitch about needing change and I agreed with her some that life could be more exciting, but then we were on the Moon, and there were plenty of nice things to it even if the organization was stifling.

Now, she looked at me like I was crazy.

"I'm talking about revolution here," she said. "We can't fix what we've got to fix by making things exciting for adrenaline junkie pilots. Life isn't a goddamned thrill ride, it's a serious goddamned thing."

I said that was true and a beautiful thing too, even if sometimes things could get a little loosened up so we could enjoy the experience of it.

"Now," she said, "all you're talking about is excitement and aesthetics. How things feel and how things look."

I said that was somewhat close to being right. Got her ticked off.

She told me that the Moon was being colonized. That the astronauts were all dead white men and the rockets had been built by Nazis to bomb London, and then those same Nazis had gone to Florida to build the rockets that first got to the Moon. She acted like this was all novel information, and I suppose to her it was.

"So, can you in good conscience talk about how exciting and beautiful everything is when you are living on land that isn't rightfully even human land that you only managed to get to because of Nazi war criminals?"

"Well, it isn't all exciting. And we got to the Moon, didn't we?" I asked.

"But you got here in the worst way. It's exploitation and violence all the way down."

"You came here the same way I did."

"I'm here to change things, you're here to rationalize them. This whole system," she said, waving her arms and the flier, "it's something that can't stand. Everything it does, it does by standing on somebody else's back."

"But, we still got to the Moon," I said, "and I suppose that amounts to something more than whatever went into the getting there. Watching the Green Spot out over the Sea of Tranquility, that's like," and this was the first time I'd ever put this feeling I'd had into words, "like knowing there's an order to things, and a beautiful one, and even the bad things have got to serve it."

Well, that still pissed her off, and she gave up on talking to me. I flew her that hop, and a few more after, but eventually she gave up and went back down.

I watched her rocket arc across the black sky until it was in front of the Green Spot and became a dot against the blue of the oceans and the green and the brown of the land.

2

A WHOLE OLD WORLD

GOLGI APPARATUS

For a very long time, there was nothing. No colonies, no warlords, no empires, and no agency—such was the ever-lasting spell of the Monroe Doctrine. Any exodus of the first world, any attempt to reinstall any semblance of organized society abroad was treated universally by the Anglo-American world the same way local attempts at these things always were—little Libyas, little Wacos: aggressive force applied not to install empire but to maintain its tortured inversion.

But it is according to the predilections of the Gods that all things good or ill should come to an end, and though this narrow modern period may sometimes have felt an eternity, it would be anything but. As the stalwart bureaucracies and institutions of the West began to fail even to police themselves, there came a moment, a Plymouth, in which an Outriding could not be reduced to the will of the 'global community.' A myriad of little cultures—boyish warbands, tech-startups, insular neo-Amish enclaves—followed, tepid at first... and brazen at last. The informal invasion of the dark continent had begun. Africa's second colonization.

In the west, along the Gold Coast, blossomed modern hubs of global trade—neo-Singapores whose markets brimmed with all the goods the old world could offer and more: an ever increasing variety of scientific wonders and exotic spectacles. Its rulers—CEO monarchs and eccentric proprietors—formed a technological elite like perhaps none in history: entire populations turned to face beaming utopias by the unitary pet projects of their personalistic, tech-bro caesars.

In Conakry, a solitary genius known only as the Master rules through a network of undying mechanical servants—kept alive, some whisper, through a twisted Kabbalistic occultism optimized in a laboratory. In Dakar, whole economic spheres have been mandated by the Company—a neo-feudal, neo-Spartan corporate state—to serve only the colonization of space. There *will* be forests on the moon, they *are* already paid for, they *are* under construction. Thirty thousand men have died.

The soldiers of Monrovia need not settle for but a single life to give for their country. Limbs, organs, flesh: all can be replaced as needed for truly unyielding berserkers whose lives can be stretched like drums across centuries. Her greatest warriors can no longer feel the wind on their faces... but the fury of battle will live inside them forever.

These bastions of enterprise—and a dozen still—hold aloft the Faustian heritage of the West, tempting Prometheus for each and every little secret they can wring from him. Their scholarship, wealth, and engineering make them mighty... but they fear as well. For just to the east of this silicon promised land lies the great flats upon which ride a new menace to civilization. Their mechanical beasts crash like torrential waves against the walls of the western cities, swelling and receding whimsically by the demands of their auguries and gods.

I speak of course of the Khanates of sand and steel. Fanatically driven by their love of car and train and bike—and anything else which rides like a stallion across blistering sands and wind swept Serengeti—they do not build cities nor construct abodes. Instead, they undulate across the mid-Saharan plains in fleets of iron and oil in a never-ending, violent pilgrimage to their gods of open sky; a quasi-primitivist, neo-pagan menace continually reconstituted in an endless stream of momentary political unions and loyal-to-the-death familial tribes. Their force is never long-lasting, but always brutal and swift. Timbuktu, a new Samarkand, bridges the two worlds; the commercial center of a continent, re-conquered over and over again by madmen whose new-found riches destroy them in a generation.

Not so south of the jungle, where generations form the brick and mortar of life itself and the roads terminate not with a sunset, but with a warm hearth tucked safely away behind grey walls patrolled by civilian sentries. These are the Covenants, a network of fortified little towns dotting much of the southern half of the continent. Each one simultaneously a contract and a kind of family, their streets are thronged with the laughter of children and their orchards and yards bustle with feasts of saintly dedication. Born of the brine of 100,000 little invasions, they hold unwaveringly to the borderer dream: government is ordained firstly by the grace of God, and lastly by the signature of a free man. When a Covenanter dies, they bake him into a brick and add him to their towering wall of ashen rock where he can *Hold the Line* for his wife and children even in death.

Perhaps you are not impressed. Perhaps you see in all this only the squirming of merchant technocrats, the drunken haze of barbarians, or the placid mediocrity of small farmers. I avail you then: Sometime in the 21st century Ethiopia fell to Mormon privateers. The most civilized of all African nations, they saw in it the grounds for something new and great. Now New Deseret holds strong from the ports of Alexandria to the wasted plains of Kenya, its imperial capital of Addis Ababa gleaming like the rising sun over the dunes that flank the Nile. All bow before the Emperor and his golden knights, the strongest men the world over—whose bronze skin glisten almost as their liege's crown of golden wreaths. Only by slaying a knight in single combat can a man join their ranks, and so the most powerful brawn of earth flocks to this mecca to face a sword of the Red Emperor; the dream of every boy to grasp one in his palm.

In each of these worlds is preserved something of ours so that even in the death of the West, of its boundless global vision, there lives on a spirit fractal in its boundless multiplicity. Perhaps one day the ruins of an America—ancient and forgotten—will be erected again. An old world made new for men once more ready for its task.

3

PHENOMENA #1740

DILLON HAMILTON

A few years into the conflict, they began to take the hands and heads of the dead so that they could not rap their knuckles against the walls of their graves and speak among themselves in the night. Some of the first that they had buried, they buried them in bitterness and left the sites unmarked and the killings unrecorded. During full moons, the blood most unjustifiably spilled cried out the loudest.

Slate had never heard the raps and voices, but tonight was his first full moon shift for the Seismic Department, since it had come under the purview of the Agency for Archeological Phenomena. The old world that had passed away had been systematically buried by the new world, and the new world found it necessary to augment existing bureaucracies to make sure that the old world remained buried.

Slate knew little about the intricacies behind the technology that he operated. He was not paid and well-kept for his knowledge, but for his record keeping. All he knew was that sensors below him were sending sound to the headphones on him. He seated himself at the Seismic Researcher's desk on this full moon night and recorded what follows, being precise at the depths from which they came.

Three raps at six feet.

Two raps at twelve feet.

Rustling at surface.

"I think I have a count," at six feet.

"What's the count?" at twelve feet.

"Seven," at six feet.

"Seems significant," at twelve feet.

"I'm completely confounded," at six feet.

"Seven is the number of completion," at twelve feet.

Rustling and grunting at surface.

"What did you say?" at twelve feet.

"Nothing. That seemed to come from above," at six feet.

"Is there another?" at twelve feet.

"There must be. I've often wondered if there were others," at six feet.

"Ask who it is," at twelve feet.

"Do we really want to know?" at six feet.

"Yes. They must be one of us to have been buried in this place," at twelve feet.

"Hello up there!" at six feet.

No answer.

"Hello up there!" at six feet.

"Hello up there!" at twelve feet.

"Hello. Do you hear it?" at surface.

"Hear what? Who are you?" at twelve feet.

"The rumbling from deep. You said your count was seven?" at surface.

"Yes," at six feet.

"Seven what?" at surface.

"Seven other femur bones. They are distinct because they are all different lengths," at six feet.

"They are the last seven," at surface.

"The last seven?" at twelve feet.

"The last seven women he bedded before his death. Was it in the space of a week?" at surface.

"Yes, it was," at six feet.

"Had you done that before?" at surface.

"No," at six feet.

"That's because they made it happen," at surface.

"Who is 'they'?" at six feet.

"Whoever put you where you are now. You'll never know their names, but they made sure that all seven of those femurs were infected with something potent. Instead of taking a bone from you, those poor girls were forced to give you one back," at surface.

"If they used such a thing against him, they must have used a similar tactic with me," twelve feet.

"That's what they used against you," surface.

"What?" twelve feet.

Disturbance from below. Depth unattained.

"They let your fear and pure rationalism drive you into deep layers of bitterness and isolation. You reclused. You thought you might be protected, but an isolated man has no one to cover for the one mistake that the enemy is waiting for him to make," surface.

Prolonged disturbance from below. Gaining intensity. Depth unattained.

"What is that below us?" six feet.

"Don't you mean 'who'?" surface.

"They bury men that deep?" twelve feet.

"They buried him that deep because they feared him most. It's not even him that rests there, but a plaque bearing his name and the title 'The Theocrat'," surface.

"Never heard of him," six feet.

"That's because he lived in the era before you—a period of gentle genocide," surface.

"The disdain one must have to go through such expense to bury even his name at unreachable depths," twelve feet.

"They didn't even bury him themselves. They convinced those closest to him to do it for them," surface.

"How is this even possible? There must have been one against it," six feet.

"There were a few over a baker's dozen, but what is a baker's dozen in the middle of Babylon?" surface.

"They were going after any politician in those days," twelve feet.

"He was no politician. He owned a small business and dared to invoke the character of God before a city council. They rezoned him, inspected him weekly, and took his millstone away. It's what killed him. Now, they are worried the

millstone will rise from the deep with him and be hung around their necks," surface.

"How do you know all of this?" six feet.

"Who are you?" twelve feet.

"I reported on each of your stories on the counterterrorism desk," surface.

"Are you at the surface? Among the living?" six feet.

"They walk past me. I offer them words that may help them live, but they do not hear me. Their ears are tuned for words that lead them to the slaughter," surface.

"Why are you buried at the surface?" twelve feet.

"They were least afraid of me and my god, who only has enough weight and glory to reside on the surface. It's our gods that they wish to bury more than it is us," surface.

Disturbance. Removed headphones momentarily. Ears ringing.

"His blood cries for him, even though the memory of him has passed," surface.

Phenomena #1740. SD—Researcher's Desk 12. Depth Range: Surface-Unknown. Researcher Slate Tunnell. Shift #40.

4

THE MACHINE

MOG THE URBANITE

"I don't understand," the boy said, staring up at the thing in the case.

"It's a trophy of conquest. Why else would it be in here?" his brother said, with all the gravitas two extra years of age gave him.

"It's not like the others," the boy answered.

It was, in fact, nothing like the other pieces in the hallway.

Tanned hides, in all shades, covered every bare piece of rock, some with tattoos, many bare. Between this grim decoupage, cases with familiar and strange weapons were littered. The hall was long, with stone walls that stretched well over their heads, but it was still crowded with trophies of conquest.

Each one had a small golden plate, explaining what it was—"The Skin of Senator Molembek," "Warhead from a Minuteman Missile," "The Pistol of Lord McCromber"—except the case they stood before.

"Maybe it's another weapon," his brother said, peering at the object behind the glass.

"How could it be?"

That was a fair question. It certainly looked nothing like a weapon. If anything, it looked like an instrument. Clearly ancient, the fine wood grain was cracked and twisted with age. There were empty spaces where strings might have once rested.

The boy peered closer.

"I think it says something. On that little square patch. I can't read it."

His brother pushed his nose against the glass, staring. "Look, it is a weapon. I can't make out the rest, but it says 'kills'. It has to be a weapon of some kind. Why else would grandfather have it here?"

Greatly daring, the boy opened the glass case. He reached in and took the aged guitar gently by the neck.

"Grandfather is going to have you beaten!" his brother warned.

"No, he won't. Father always said the Warlord loves boldness. Now, here, look at it closer."

The two boys read the faded label on the trophy.

"I don't understand," the elder brother finally admitted.

Behind him, the boy heard the sound of footsteps on stone. Hurriedly, his earlier words forgotten, he set the guitar in its case.

Later, as they walked towards the throne room, the two boys talked about the strange trophy.

"I have no idea what a 'fascist' is supposed to be. Much less how that thing could kill one," the younger one said.

His brother shrugged. It didn't make sense to him either.

5

SINS OF THE FATHERS

P.C.M. CHRIST

"Darling, you must choose. Choose life. Choose the future. Choose Harrison and me."

"Mary, Tyler is my son. I have two. You have two."

"Not for long we don't."

Chris sighed, knowing she was right. Harrison, his firstborn, was everything a parent could hope for. Healthy, smart, handsome, well-mannered, charming, athletic. Like his father and mother, he was exemplary in every way. Yet, due to the cruelty of cosmic injustice, the imperfection of the genetic lottery, who knows, Tyler, their second child, was a mockery of every concept of evolution. Half-formed and hideous, he was also crippled by various mental disorders that had on many occasion led him to outbursts of violence, and all with an intelligence nearing that of a vegetative state. Simply put, he never would have survived birth nor life without the technology of the day, and was forced to live his life as such.

More tragic still was the weight his being had placed on his family. For almost a century now, a eugenics program had been implemented to ensure the robustness of citizens and, thereby, civilization itself. Parents of tragedies such as Tyler were forced to witness a life that could never recover from its handicaps, its disorders and/or diseases, perhaps its nature. But to bear such a burden unnecessarily?

"I need some time, Mary."

"You have less than half an hour," Mary reminded. She rubbed his shoulder for what she did not know would be the last time and walked out to the front room to wait.

Regardless of the parents' decision, the child would be removed. The choice for the parents was whether or not they would join their handicapped child outside civilization.

Mary had made her choice.

Chris sat in the bedroom weighing it all, the morals, the ethics, the tradition, the expectations, the shame until Mary called saying the officers had arrived.

He walked out to where Tyler sat in the chair drooling, screaming occasionally, flicking his own ear to the point of pain, a bandage around his arm where he had bit himself, a backpack of medicine beside him.

"I'm going with Tyler."

He attempted to announce this with moral dignity, but Mary looked at him aghast, ashamed that he would make such a choice, the waste, the rejection of his fine lot in life of which she was most certainly a part. She turned and never looked back.

He and the boy were removed without ceremony and driven in a small shuttle to a gated encampment far from the city.

A mass of bare flesh swarmed over them as they entered. Tears accompanied each embrace, both given freely, the stench of unwashed humanity blending with the dirt and grass around them.

Tyler was led to the children's area as Chris was given a brief orientation.

After being told to remove his clothes, he walked with Mother.

"Our way of living is communal. Care, sex, love; all are given freely and broadly. One must 'leave themselves at the door.' We do not allow outliers. We do not allow any to be above another."

"What about healthy children?"

"We do not say healthy. Some privileged children have been brought in as siblings of those with special needs. If they are not disabled in some way, they must be taught all-encompassing empathy, to view the world as a disabled person would. This is made easier by their relation to those who need them most. There are, of course, some accidental births through penial and vaginal intercourse. Those who have not been able to adapt to our way of life sometimes commit suicide, which, frankly, is for the best. Some attempt escape, but are rarely successful. But, truly, what is waiting for them out there?"

"A family?" He had said it without thinking. He missed Mary. He missed Harrison.

"We are your family now. There is one sin in this community, and it is unforgivable—that you would place yourself above the group. If we are to be the bosom for the weak, then we must be strong, and we can only be strong together. I'll be frank, what is built out of weakness cannot stand on its own, and there will be swift and unrelenting punishment for any who would dare risk our safety. There is no greater priority for those who cannot defend themselves."

"Why not allow them a choice?"

"There is no choice when it comes to doing what is right. There is dignity in failure. We celebrate our imperfections because we are them. This is how we grow. You are either imperfect or you live for those who are."

Time passed, and Chris grew accustomed to the way of life. Tyler never changed, never bettered, only growing more and more demanding, he and the other invalids terrorizing the community, who endured with a grin and wry smile, their love based on one's tolerance for suffering, righteousness through pain, gratitude for the hobbling weight of a cross to bear.

At six months, and to community-wide celebration, Chris began lactating—a sign, he was told, of his growing empathy, his body accepting its place as nurturer. The old ways, the old him were left behind. He was now one of them.

As if Earth itself wished to offer a gift, on that day the main gate opened, and a father and mother stood there with their daughter incapacitated by Down syndrome—and to the surprise of all, had brought along their son, a perfectly healthy and capable boy.

Chris and the others cried tears of joy and understanding as they reached for the family, grasping, pulling them close, the heat of their bodies added to the mass. They were so lost, so alone, so in need of love, so ready to help. They would be welcomed freely with open arms, pulled tight to offered breasts, suck and want no more.

6

GOOD NEWS, FAKE NEWS

EOR ODINSON

hey u up?

this shit crazy

Yeah

I have CNN on right now

But it's on every channel

cnn r u serious rn?

at least find a stream

i can link u 1 if u want

I can't believe they actually did it

They hit the button

They really did it

God save us

no man its fake

its all fake man nukes arent real

its a psyop

if bombs were dropping they wouldn't

just sit there and tell us lmao

they would be in the bunkers man

we wud be on our own

Are you hearing this stuff about interceptions?

ya there some spooky shit goin on

what r they saying on cnn?

They say there are unknown craft

They say they are intercepting the missles

Now they are arguing

Someone is saying that we launched AT the craft

Not at each other

its a psyop man

if they say that we fired @ ufos

then it was WW3 and ayys are saving us

if they say that ayys are saving us

then its project blue beans

*beam

They have a guy on now

He says this may be Israel

A secret extension of the iron dome

They are saving us after all we did

lmao dude

smdh

im trying to send a video

but they keep taking it down

What is it?

its a huge fking ship

a ufo

its bluebeam its gotta b

Where are you getting this from?

from /pol/

Huh?

from 4chan

Why are you wasting your time on there

Especially now

You're crazy!

dude there are anons all over

i saw a video of lights in siberia

and kansas

a guy shot at one

another guy sent up some balloons

with helium and some with his piss

and a note

fuck off were full

lol

The President is on CNN

He says that the craft have saved us

Saved us from ourselves

My God, he said Jesus is with them!!!

ok taht seals it

fake ass bluebeam

next they will say iron man

then harry potter and shit

they are setting up nwo

thats endgame

We're surrendering

All of Earth

We're going to let them lead us

Finally there will be peace in our time

We can even go with them

dont!!!!

do not get on 1 of those ufos

its a trap

im begging u

dude

plz respond

I love you.

7

UNDER THE WILLOW

WILLIAM WHEELWRIGHT

Charlotte was both glad of and vexed by the willow branches under which she stood. On the one hand, they provided ample cover, and she wanted to appear nonchalant upon the arrival of her beau, but on the other, with so much wind coursing through them as to almost make the moment unromantic, she was concerned that their sonorous rustling, otherwise so pacifying, would obscure the sound of his approaching footsteps, unapologetic and boisterous though they were, rendering her unprepared and thus appearing, well, shall we shall, immature, at the moment of his appearance. The truth was that she was immature, and indeed, the following day was her eighteenth birthday.

He had been gone for three whole years. This was how things were done now. At the age of eighteen the young men of the village, now considered fit for duty after nine years of training in the vicinity, leave for three years to pay service to the nation, positioned and ranked according to ability. She did not know where her William was, as it was not permitted to write home while on this excursion. But she had heard tell that he was with a patrol in the mountains along the border. He was due back that day, and she was waiting for him in the place he prescribed to her before his departure. You see, such was their romance. He, of epistolary persuasion, had never once acknowledged her in person. After all, at the time, she was prohibitively young. And furthermore, he was maniacally focused on the perfection of himself. In the gymnasium, of his body. In the library, of his mind. And in the sacristy, of his soul. Though provincial by birth, in his blood he felt a certain ulterior pulse, and it was thence that he derived his conviction of self.

She looked at the leaves of the willow. Her grandmother had told her that, before things changed, people used to think of them as sad trees. The long, pliable growths were even worn around the hats of the jilted. A wave of terror came over her, as she clutched in distressed hands the plaits of her long dress, the finest she owned, dark blue and of a fabric bedazzled all o'er with dragonflies. She clutched in a fury of worry. What if his experience of the last years had been the opposite of hers? She, who stayed up nearly every night, watching the stars in fits of anxiety over his well-being and safety. Did he not share the intensity of her feeling? Three years was a long time, and she had heard from some of the older women of the village that the minds of men were quick to wander and stray after whatever shiny object caught their fancy. (It must be noted for your sake, dear reader, that these women were, without exception, unmarried and barren.) Her head began to spin with all the horrible possibilities, worst of all that he had no intention of appearing, though she knew he would be back today, and word had been sent in advance. She became fretful, turning this way and that, and at last toward the great lake on whose bank she was standing, the wind lapping across it with ferocity, causing little waves to crash cutely on the grassy bank. She felt the urge to go out on the pier, just outside the protection of the willow, whose portent and symbol she now felt she was beginning to understand as the evening went down further into the west with every passing moment.

She turned to rush toward the pier, half a mind to cast herself in and let herself be drowned when, there he was, in all his radiance, his gleaming skin inexplicably clean after his ride from the mountains, his blond hair rivaling hers for length, his body twice as built as the last time she saw him, when he had nevertheless been the strongest lad in the village. She diverted her run, initially intended for the pier, towards him, although half with fury, as she blamed him for the state into which she had just worked herself at his absence. Despite their three-year separation, and really their total lack of connection before that, he seemed to perfectly understand the state of her mind, and, adjusting his body to accommodate it, he relieved himself of his heavy pack and received her embrace into his arms.

"William!" she sighed, her tears flowing, not yet undistracted by her grief.

"No, it's not William. It's Geoffrey, William's younger brother. Charlotte, William is not coming. He was killed yesterday by a rebel potshot from the mountains."

She imagined it to be a practical joke William was playing. After all, she did not know his character; perhaps this behavior was within it. She wiped her tears away and smiled, laughing at the humorous joke. With the huge emotional fluctuation she was practically delirious, and she moved to kiss Geoffrey.

Without speech, he evaded her advance, and shook her, prompting her to look at his eyes.

She looked at them, wherein she encountered the most horrible gravity, made all the more solemn by their want of tears. The realization overtaking her, her knees buckled, and the saltwater ran unabated down her reddened cheeks between ghastly sobs and inhalations of phlegm.

Geoffrey, not knowing what else to do, left her alone there, returning over the hill, to the village.

She wept there in a heap as the night grew dark. Turning over she saw the look of the willow leaves in the moonlight, made a broken crystalline in her flooded eyes.

8

THE WIND THAT SHAKES THE PALMS

ARBOGAST

The Federals were slick with sweat. A permanent coating of grease that made each man uncomfortable, even those among them accustomed to the tropics. The agent in charge of the mission, codenamed Reaper, kept swearing under his breath as he counted the small team assembled on the night beach. Reaper did not like the fact that the government, or rather what was left of it, had only provided him with eleven men. They blamed budget constraints, per usual. Despite this, they fully expected Reaper and his team to take out and take down the entire island of New Providence with alacrity.

"Send us a recorded brief when it is done," was all the FBI CIO had said via FaceTime from his secure location somewhere outside of Ottawa.

Reaper had been with the FBI since the beginning of The Turbulence, and never once had he seen the bureau acknowledge that they were losing. The higher-ups continued to see the war as the prolonged bellyaching of backwater losers upset over misinformation. No one, especially not the president-in-exile, could face the fact that a majority of states had convened, nominated a new government, and had forged a new path without them. The bureau made hay out of the early victories in New York, California, and Illinois, all the while ignoring the major defeats in New Hampshire, Maryland, and the humiliating siege of Morgantown, West Virginia.

The bureau just could not let it go and concede defeat, so Reaper and his team of new fish were down in the Bay Islands, trying to arrest a bunch of Neo-Puritan privateers from all across the US. The purpose was to harass the small rouge bands that had popped up since the return of Letters of Marque, and the bureau thought that eliminating religious fanatics would be good optics. Reaper had to laugh because he knew that the Neo-Puritans had been invited in by the English-speaking residents, almost all of whom badly wanted to break away from Honduras and her Spanish-speaking mestizos.

Reaper motioned for his team to move to the first series of checkpoints. From the beach, the team, dressed all in black, moved to a collection of bungalows that had once belonged to a British tourism company. Intelligence reported that the Neo-Puritans had turned the bungalows into blockhouses each manned by a rifleman. At the count of three, Reaper signalled for the team to open fire. A series of short, sharp bursts echoed across the sultry night. Small fires from the M-4 carbines looked like fireflies. After ten seconds, a ceasefire was called. The Federals had not received return fire. The bungalows proved to be empty.

The team passed the bungalows and moved into an open area of palm trees and sand. To the northwest stood a luxury hotel. To the east, a bar that had once catered to swingers but now was the de-facto headquarters of the privateers. Reaper decided to split the team up and move on both targets simultaneously. Within seconds, one of the Federals was struck by a small pistol round, possibly a 9mm, that lodged in his upper thigh. The ill-disciplined Federals fired wildly at the unseen shooter, thus giving away their location. Reaper tried to correct them, but it was too late. Small arms fire came from behind palm trees and from the darkened bar. Even worse, a sniper firing from a hotel balcony managed to incapacitate three of Reaper's men. All the Federals could do was spray and pray. As in Vietnam and other misadventures, the tactics did nothing. Reaper began to panic when he realized that he was the only Federal left alive and unscathed.

"Nice try, Revenue Agent. It was a good show, although all too short."

The voice belonged to Amos Winthrop, the nom de plume of the former far-right radical Chris Pelligrew. Few characters of The Turbulence were as loathed by the bureau as Winthrop, a free man only because of a shock pardon by the governor of Virginia. Despite his claims of conversion, the FBI considered him nothing less than an unrepentant Nazi. Now, one of the bureau's veteran agents had to swallow the fact that Winthrop could decide his fate.

"Sad that the Hondurans gave us a tougher fight than you lot. I guess the West really has fallen." Winthrop's comment elicited laughter from his men.

"I think it would be wise if you stood up from the grass and surrendered, agent. We will not harm you. In fact, if you are so inclined, we would like to offer you a position with our merry band. Only thing you need is faith in Our Lord and the Good Word. Do you believe in God, sir?"

Reaper clenched his teeth. Although not mandatory, radical atheism had become standard at the bureau since the defection of the Mormons. Reaper had gone to church as a child, but government work had turned him away from Christ.

"Can't say that I do," Reaper responded.

"Pity then. Maybe you can learn to love Him from one of the most beautiful places he created." The mouth of a pistol was placed behind Reaper's ear. The federal agent stood up and saw the man holding it. Winthrop smiled crookedly at him, held out his hand, offered to escort Reaper to his new prison: a first-floor room inside of the luxury hotel. Reaper prepared himself for a lifetime of repeating only his name, ID, and Social Security number. He hoped that a rescue mission would at least be attempted. His lone fear was Stockholm syndrome, whereby he would become a Roundhead corsair consumed by drinking, praying, and fighting.

In Ottawa, the Director of the FBI heard news of the raid's failure. He signed a document stating that Reaper was dead. This set in motion a series of emails, one of which would reach the Reaper's estranged wife. No rescue mission would ever be planned.

9

RECONQUISTA

LOMEZ

"On the right hand of the Indies, there is an island called California, very close to the side of the Terrestrial Paradise, peopled by a race of giant golden-tanned women living in the fashion of Amazons. They are of strong and hard bodies, of ardent courage and force. Their island is the strongest in all of the world, with its steep cliffs and rocky shores. Their arms are all of gold, and so are the harnesses of the majestic beasts they have tamed and ride, for on the whole of their island of California, there is no metal but gold."

—GARCI RODRÍGUEZ DE MONTALVO,
LAS SERGAS DE ESPLANDIÁN (1508)

The depleted company calling themselves the Cali-Yuga made camp at a bonfire pit on a wide-open stretch of empty beach with the briny sweet smell of misty Pacific Ocean air filling up their lungs. The bluff behind them was dotted in opulent seaside mansions, all concrete and glass, built in the era of fanatical decadence now brought to a bloody and brutal end by the war, and whose wall-size picture windows returned the setting sunlight back across the burning sky. Each soldier could have claimed one of the empty mansions for himself, and perhaps soon would, but for tonight the men would celebrate together on the beach.

They had spent the day marching west from Corona where they'd fought their last battle, and likely the final battle of the war, two days before. Their final objective had been to clear and sweep remaining enemy encampments along the 91W corridor between I-15 and the coastline, but it had been a quiet two days, the enemy dead or scattered eastward like dried leaves to the gale-force Santa Anas ripping through the palms.

Some of the men swam in the choppy surf while others gathered driftwood to make fires and prep the public grills, sooty and long neglected and covered in seagull shit but plenty suitable for the stocks of meats and produce taken earlier that afternoon from an abandoned Gelson's freezer room, while others stood in the cold wet sand of the foreshore, pants rolled to their knees, the lapping water locking around their swollen and tired feet and then folding back again into the surf, the men like monuments in a row looking up and down the shoreline unobstructed for miles and miles south and north until the misty air made a blur of the sightline, and west over the wind-capped ocean to the adumbrated rump of Catalina, realizing for the first time that their dream of coming home, of taking back what was theirs, every last square inch of it, from San Diego to Shasta, the birthplace of their grandfathers, a dream they'd held at a distance for generations because of its seeming impossibility, finally, after all of these years of helplessness and relentless longing, was not a dream at all.

Their leader was Captain Tom Sepúlveda. Big Tom, they called him. He had been born Thomas Cole, after the painter, in a small town in eastern Oregon but according to (likely apocryphal) family lore traced his lineage back to the great Californio patriarch Francisco Xavier Sepúlveda who had settled much of Los Angeles in the late 1700's and whose immediate descendants had fought alongside the Bear Flaggers and Commodore Robert F. Stockton to claim California from the Mexicans nearly a century later.

Big Tom, in his 50's, achy from the two-day march from the desert, smoked a cigarillo and drank from a jennie of 2019 Screaming Eagle commemorating the last year a Cole-Sepúlveda had lived in California and which he'd been saving his entire adulthood for just this moment. The wine was woody and in its advanced age had ripened to a flavor of gamy stew. It reminded him of the kind of thing he might have eaten as a boy with his father after a winter deer hunt along the Grande Ronde. He relished every sip.

While the men feasted and drank and the plasma streaks of last light gave way to coming night, Big Tom coordinated on his radio with the rest of the infantry division garrisoned in various locations up and down the state. The bases at Beale, Travis, Edwards, and finally Vandenberg had all been secured. The militias from the State of Jefferson were still engaged in low-level gunfights with holdout cartels in Humboldt County but otherwise had control of every major chokepoint and supply route north of Sacramento. For their efforts, the State of Jefferson would annex everything south to the Alpine County border on the east and the border of Mendocino County on the west. The new NorCal Republic would govern everything south of there to the edge of Monterey in a straight line across the state to the Inyo-Nevada border. Finally, New California, the Golden Land, the Terrestrial Paradise, including Captain Big Tom Sepúlveda and the men of the Cali-Yuga, would occupy the rest.

Part of Big Tom's family lore rested on a box of insurance paperwork and photos of buildings destroyed in the 1989 earthquake and presumed to have at one time belonged to the family. As a kid, Tom obsessively studied these photos with a morbid fascination that was only now coming into focus. The history of California was the history of cataclysmic tectonic shifts, and though Big Tom had never experienced an earthquake, not as a kid and not yet as a man, he knew them in his bones and blood. He understood their nature. He understood the lifetime scale of slowly accumulating pressures. He understood that while on the surface what you saw was an enigma of weird and random fissures, and what you felt was the sudden and unpredictable explosions of bedrock earth, deep down underneath your feet the big plates at the geological scale were always moving steadily and inexorably in a single direction. He understood that geological time and human time are two different things, but they are always converging, and when they do we call it history.

10

BLOOD TIES

MYTHPILOT

"Do you think we're doing the right thing?"

"Of course we are. This is the way things have to be now. It's peace for our time."

"I mean by them." The woman removes her jewelry piece by piece. Her earrings and necklace click individually as she sets them down on the bureau's glassy expanse of counter-enameled crystal in this welcome muffle of their apartment, the festivities still ringing in her ears.

Her husband has removed his shoes. His chief adjutant's ghostlike presence has been finally banished; barring emergency, there will be no more audiences, dispatches, huddles, dictations, favors to grant, or decisions for the night. The grand thing is in motion and he stretches his long lean frame into a grateful angle of repose. She admires him now at rest. How rarely in the last several years has the public even seen him seated? She once again appreciates their intimacy, now more than ever.

Now he stands again, his hands on her shoulders, planting a kiss on her upturned cheek. "You want to be reassured? You yourself wrote the open letter. It was magnificent, Anna. Queenlike. And ten years later, here we are."

"Biopolitics." She smiles at the memory. "But particularly more gracefully expressed. 'The return of grand romance.' I did, didn't I. We were much younger then. Everything we wanted to achieve, it seemed like a dream. But also..." She stretches sleepily, searching for the right word. "Also imminent. It was all just within reach."

She continues: "You know it's different now though. To see your daughter leave home, I mean. Of course I knew she would, one day. All daughters leave. But to the Russians? It's just so far—and don't talk to me about your rockets, I know that soon, if all stays on track, we could be in Moscow in two hours if we wanted. It's the conceptual distance. These are the people who bombed us, James."

"That was a long time ago. We did the same to them." The memory of that long scrabble upwards, through so many decades of rebuilding, and fighting, and politiquing—it all flits across his face, deepening his forehead lines and the wrinkles around his lips as if he was momentarily weighted down again by those billions of tons of soot-caked rubble. The ruin of the Old World.

"I know this too. I don't blame them at all. It's just a mother's heart."

"Well, we gained a son too. I knew Prince Ivan was an impressive young man, but now I'm even more reassured that it was closer to an even trade, although I think our Elizabeth counts double. Eldest for eldest. Fair, if I can set aside my bias for a moment. He'll do well here. I'm putting him to work on rebuilding New York."

"Kitty is delighted with him. She really is. You know she showed me some of their letters? They're really very sweet."

James allows himself to be hopeful for a moment, but not without a touch of cynicism. "Now we can all call off the fucking submarines, thank God." Those had really been the cruelest. A second war, about ten years after the first. Zombie nations without even anything to bomb, but still a few weapons left, deep underwater, fueled by pure spite. They let them fly, and snuffed out their infant hopes. But even this was a long time ago. Tonight is not for mourning; it is for life itself. James lifts his chin, as he so often had when addressing his people.

"It's a new world, darling, and it belongs to us. We used to trust pieces of paper for peace. Now we trust blood. That's it. That's all. That's all there ever was. Peace has a price. Blood for blood. You always pay in blood. Sometimes sooner, sometimes later, but you always pay."

He continues: "But... people forgot there was an easy way to do it. *You don't have to go to war*. You can pay up front. Exchange of persons. Daughters for sons. What world leader would ever push the button again knowing his children might be within the blast radius? That's how we make peace. They used to think this was barbarous. They preferred to bomb each other instead, and of course their politics didn't even allow for essential persons. The whole point was to get the *human* out of the machine. No one allowed to *do* anything, except sleepwalk into war. No wonder they abolished themselves."

Anna sees the beginning of a fine speech in her husband's musings. "Well, despite my mother-sadness, I think it's a marvelous thing. Blood is *human*, blood is *warm*, blood is *us*. This can be the beginning of a new age, a *human* age. It really can, James."

Now James takes his wife by the hand to the balcony, a wide promontory soaring out from the graceful, vertical, and deliberately self-confident Reconstruction style. No more bunkers. He turns her on the marble floor and shows her the fireworks over a re-built city twinkling with lights.

"This time we trust *people* for our peace. Ourselves, our new *Russian* family, two very special young couples. Agreements between families, agreements between nations. *Men* rule, paper doesn't. Tonight we're back, Anna. We're back forever. It's the beginning of something really new; this empty earth can be an Eden. Tonight the old world is banished. It's *ours* now."

11

POW/MIA 2035

PINEWALKER

Slowly, slowly, walk the path
And you might never stumble or fall
Slowly, slowly, walk the path
And you might never fall in love at all

When the tourniquet was tight he crawled up to the crest of a little ridge and leaned against a spruce tree, gazing at the setting sun. No cell reception out here, but he pulled out his phone and listened to a song he'd downloaded earlier that reminded him of his childhood, from a Scottish folk band called Silly Wizard. The morphine had dulled the pain, while the dex he'd taken before he set out kept it from completely dulling his mind. He felt chilled and tired. It didn't hurt anymore but he was fully aware of what little remained of his left leg. There were a half dozen smaller shrapnel wounds that he barely even noticed—they weren't what would kill him.

Thermal-equipped helicopters are a bitch. He'd been asked to go solo—the north woods were a clusterfuck of guerrilla fighting and they'd gotten info on someone important. He did it with a good suppressed rifle. By the time the guards realized what was going on, one was choking on his own blood and both the VIP and a radio technician were splayed awkwardly on the ground. They must have called in air support after that. He probably missed those last moving potshots at the radio equipment. Or they had Starlink. Doesn't matter now, it's over.

Golden, golden, is her hair
Like the morning sun over fields of corn
Golden, golden, flows her love
So sweet and clear and warm

He'd done this for her, he reminded himself. Made a vow. One hundred acres, no less, and I'll build a cabin. "I'll give you as many children as you can give me," he said, before he kissed her forehead. She fixed him with those ocean-green eyes, the green he'd only see in the Gulf of Maine where the salt air smells like nowhere else. She asked him, "You promise?" and he answered with another kiss. He went solid gold for the engagement rings. Maybe an archaeologist would find his.

He made it eleven miles out of twenty-four before the gunship found him. Search and rescue was hard enough in peacetime, impossible at war. Sometimes hikers died in the White Mountains and all that's found are the metal parts: belt buckles, backpack frames. Larger animals would eat the flesh, and the mice would nibble the bones and fabrics down. Those stories were before synthetics and GPS were so ubiquitous though, and the rifle would survive a while. But she might never know what happened to him.

Lonely, lonely, is the heart
That ne'er another can call its own
Lonely, lonely lies the part
That has to live all alone

One last cigarette. He always kept three in the little pocket on the arm of his jacket. Hand them out to friends, burn one on a late watch. He'd given one to old Timmy, with his intestines laid out—the bullet had hit him sideways and then ricocheted off his plates from the inside and opened him up. Held the hand of his old bos'n from the trawler while he slipped off, and cried like a bitch afterwards. Nick caught one to the head and just went lights out. He'd smoked all three before putting the two silver dollars in his wallet over Nick's eyes. A toll for the ferryman, and a damn good one at $80/oz.

Wildly, wildly, beats the heart
With a rush of love like a mountain stream
Wildly, wildly, play your part
As free as a wild bird's dream

Sarah. I'm sorry for your soul, the sins I led you to. Our liaisons in the woods—the nights were too lonely. I never confessed at mass; you did. I'm so sorry. I couldn't wait for you, pale and pure under the moonlight. Will you end up in one of the camps in Massachusetts? What if you're pregnant? God forgive me for what I've done, how I've left you. I wish I could see you again one last time, feel you on my skin, hold you closer than I ever held anyone else. Your breath on my neck. The smell of your hair. The things I did for your future. God forgive me.

He cut the tourniquet off. As blood stained the moss he saw a vision of smoke rising from a cabin. Tall pines. Green water, fishermen cheering at cod hauled up on lines of hooks. His father's face. Woodstoves in winter. Blood and terror and love, and then everything went brilliantly white as the sun fell behind the ridge. He threw his dog tags as far as he could with the last of his strength before he became one with the earth again.

Golden, golden, is her hair
Like the morning sun over fields of corn
Golden, golden, is her love
So sweet and clear and warm

Henry Kowalczyk sat on the bench in the locker room. Eight hours duty at the Tomb of the Unknown Soldier in Manchester, United Atlantic States. There used to be a casino here; now there's a graveyard with marble columns. He texted Mom, told her that he'd be home soon. She'd have perogies waiting for him, with sour cream and browned onions. He impatiently twisted the golden band on his finger. Mom insisted that he take it. He'd given a custom-made counterpart to Julia, paid by Dad's pension. The wedding was still a month away. It had been hard growing up under a single mother, but he now had something besides a uniform. A deed for 130 acres and a house in Oxbow, stamped by Admiral Conrad himself. He'd carry her across the threshold on their honeymoon, and the next day Nate would truck in twenty head of milk cow. Between that and the pension, it'd be enough to live on and then some.

He still wondered to himself—would Dad be proud of me?

12

OMELAS HAS BEEN UNJUSTLY MALIGNED

GASTON NERVAL

Someday I hope you will come to visit us in our fair city of Omelas. I hope, when you do, that you will find pleasant our broad avenues and the shade of their fragrant trees; look with admiration on our statuary and architecture; marvel at the efficiency and cleanliness of our streetcars. But most of all I hope that your visit coincides with one of the civil displays that make all of this possible.

You may have received or constructed an erroneous impression of us: that we are cruel, or (even worse) naive. It is popularly supposed that the material prosperity and social harmony which prevail in the city of Omelas do so because we, its citizens, are able to tolerate the knowledge that our society is upheld by the undeserved suffering of an innocent human being. Not so!

This mendacious calumny is a deliberate misrepresentation of our customs. When he reaches the age of majority, as the capstone of his education, each citizen is indeed taken to the presence of a tortured infant. But it is not the elders and magistrates of the city who have reduced him to this horrible state. Even in Omelas, alas, there are criminals. It could not be otherwise in a great city. He is then presented with a choice: is he willing to kill the criminal guilty of this offense?

If he is, his name is added to the register of full citizens. On the dates of our civil displays, a name is drawn by lot from this register, and its bearer is called to perform his duty. He waits, unmasked, at the top of a stair in the public circle while the condemned criminal ascends for the last time. With his own hands, he drapes a thick rope about the criminal's head, and a few moments later, drops him, killing him by breaking his neck.

If he is unwilling to take on this terrible responsibility, he is not exiled. He may continue to live in Omelas if he wishes—he is welcome to do so! But he will not be permitted to hold a position of public trust, or granted a voice in the civil assemblies of the people.

For that is justice. It is unjust for the innocent to be tortured, yes; but it is unjust too for the guilty to go unpunished. The law is that which kills. This is the tie that binds us, we citizens of Omelas. The ones who walk away from us are those who find unendurable not the suffering of the innocent but the punishment of the wicked.

The torture of children, of course, is not the only crime for which this dread punishment is ordered. Will you find it maddening if I refuse to enumerate them for you? Then perhaps you had best visit for only a short time. Not that you need fear you would be subjected to it yourself: we are a civilized people, and I promise you that any civilized man would judge them as harshly as we (or even more so). But when you visit our bright city, look about you, and think on your own.

13

THE CENSOR

WOLAND

The Great Algorithm is a beautiful web of coercion, silencing, and guided penance. It is the filter through which our lives remain sane. Yet even it is not all-seeing, all-knowing. Lies grow between its sweet eyes like bubbles. The Online Division of Freedom and Peace is necessary. It pops the lies before they float to heaven.

Ashley has been with ODFP for three years. The Algorithm sends her lies each day—well-hidden lies, smooth lies, tricky lies. Sometimes there is a truth and Ashley lets it enter the digest. Mostly, she clicks the red button. She has been clicking the red button a lot lately. A new type of lie has appeared, and the Algorithm doesn't know what to do with it.

The message awaiting her verdict reads: "Happy Birthday to Sky King, a real human bean. Let us honor him through anti-establishment, anti-capitalist action." The amalgam of memes balances the judicial scale perfectly. Human subjective analysis is necessary.

Sky King is beloved by terrorists but had not been a terrorist himself. Anti-establishment? Definitely, but in the days of confusion, before Kamala unified progress and law. Does that make him a true freedom fighter, then?

Citizen John McCoy works for Atlanta Insurance. Zero strikes on his record. His message has no likes or replies. Had it been posted on a whim or as a signal, a flare in the digital jungle to help him find friends? Is the second sentence authentic or tacked on to cover his tracks?

Ashley glances at her backlog and confirms that Sky King is present in nearly every message. Everything she knows about the meme comes from reports the Algorithm supplied. She blows a sigh, remembering last year's Bowden-inspired poetry. To decode the messages, she needs to know more. She needs the primary source material.

Ashley enters her ODFP ID into the terminal, granting her Level 2 Meme Security Clearance. The database expands beyond the public record, but "Sky King" yields nothing. She chews her fingernail in agitation. She will have to put in a special access request.

* * *

Two days later, Ashley enters a secure building in Washington, DC. A Capitol Police officer leads her to a vacant room for meme review. "You have ten minutes," he says and closes the door. Ashley turns on the projector. Gentle classical music softens her mood.

> *I'm just a broken guy who's got a few screws loose, I guess. Never really knew it until now... I don't want to hurt no one...*

The video ends with the setting sun. Lights come on and an officer escorts Ashley to the debriefing room. A tall man with hooded eyes and an earpiece greets her across a bolted metal table.

"Ashley Horgath... I hear you've been with us for three years. That's a good amount of time. How do you like it so far?"

"The work can be challenging, but it's worth the reward."

"Right, and this is your first time here. It's standard procedure. I'll ask you a few questions, then you can get on with your day. What do you think of the video?"

"It provided useful information. Now I know what Sky King is all about."

"Set work aside for a moment. How do you feel about it personally?"

"Oh, I'm not sure—I mean, obviously the man was a psychopath. The video is basically a primer on toxic masculinity."

"Why do you think he did it?"

"He was sad and alone. A stupid white guy who figured out his time had come to an end."

"He said a lot of people cared about him. He wasn't alone."

"Maybe it was the minimum wage job."

"Many people had a minimum wage job back then."

"Well, as I said, a toxic, delusional white guy. Probably a narcissist."

"Do you think you could do what he did?"

Ashley has to laugh at that. "Joyride in an airplane? No way."

"Do you feel any sympathy for him at all?"

"No."

"Good. Thank you, Ashley. I'm glad you came in today." He presses a red button on the underside of the table. Two men enter the room and bag Ashley, stifling her screams. Unfortunately, the Algorithm had detected a lie.

14

THE PASTURE

META PRIME

John pushed his chair back from the monitor and let out the sigh of someone who was no longer surprised by what he saw, but disappointed nonetheless. His five years overseeing Sheep in The Pasture was almost up and while there were many successes to celebrate, there were far more failures than one would like. This latest sigh was a result of watching yet another Sheep slowly fall sick and degenerate to a point that he might have to escalate the situation.

It would be ideal if every Sheep could graduate or, even better, transcend their lineage, but it was well known that Sheep rarely did. Even the families who were able to get their offspring placed in ideal positions in The Pasture had little hope this would make a difference. However, having a Sheep who became a Camel, or even a Lion, was a great honor and families always did everything they could to secure even the tiniest advantage. It was not that being a Camel, Lion, or even a Child afforded you a different quality of life, as everyone had all necessities taken care of, but the self-respect of proving your soul to be something more than that of your ancestors was something you could carry with you the rest of your life.

John had been born to Sheep and graduated as a Sheep himself. Not unexpected. His time in The Pasture had gone as many did, and so his first job was that of an observer, watching over the young. The idea was that by observing new souls go through the same experience and seeing where they went wrong, one could better come to understand their own mistakes and ensure they did not repeat them now that they had entered society. This had been the way for generations and had proven a successful method for educating Sheep after they left The Pasture.

John had been watching one particular Sheep whose degeneracy from sickness was particularly disturbing. He understood why this happened all too well, but it hadn't made it easier to watch. In fact, it got harder each time he witnessed another Sheep make the same mistakes he could now see coming long before they occurred. That being said, he did find himself much more grateful every time he went home to his family at the end of his shift or when he went for walks around the community to breathe in the fresh air and take in the sun. The fact that he had been blessed with such a bountiful life post-graduation, and that this life awaited all, even Sheep, helped him not feel as discouraged during his work.

Even then, you still couldn't help but feel bad when a Sheep got sick. The Sheep John had been watching was one of the sickest he had seen in his time as an observer. Time moved relatively faster in The Pasture so that the young could experience full lives before joining society. In his five-year shift, John could watch a successful soul from matriculation to graduation... if they used their full time. While The Pasture was meant to be both a learning experience and the method of judging a soul, the Children had decided that it was better to pull out a soul early if it had stopped learning, lest long-term damage be done that would impede that soul's ability to enter society.

John's work rarely required much more than simple observation—after all, The Pasture was built to run itself—but sometimes a Sheep was sick to the point of harming themselves and others. It was John's responsibility to bring this to the attention of the Children, so they could let it play out or pull the soul before irreparable damage was done.

This was one of those cases. This Sheep was so sick that it had mutilated its own body and seemed to think this an improvement from its natural form. While the physical damage a Sheep experienced was only experienced in The Pasture, the psychological damage could very well leave a scar in the Sheep's mind that persisted throughout their full life in society. There had even been rare cases where Sheep had been so badly damaged by their experience in The Pasture that they did not take on jobs in society until after years, sometimes decades of personal work.

John often felt that it was less so the awakening to society and more the shame of realizing their spiritual failure that caused the wounded souls to need so much personal work before they could come to accept themselves and be ready to give back to those around them.

While Sheep, Camels, Lions, and Children worked in society together and did not differentiate themselves by their physical appearance, Sheep who were pulled early always looked like a kid who had been caught stealing cookies and was then made to eat them in front of the whole family. They had to live with the fact that souls of their caliber had not built society but actively undermined it, and only now had the opportunity to enjoy it by the good graces of the Children, Lions, and Camels who had sacrificed before them.

John pulled his chair back to the monitor and navigated through a few control menus until he reached the option to request a review from one of the Children. He hesitated for a brief moment. The worst part would not be the Child reviewing the Sheep's status with him, but that if the Child deemed it necessary to pull the sick Sheep, the parents would have to be notified for consent. Nothing was worse than hearing your offspring was being pulled early from The Pasture.

John sighed that same sigh again and pushed the button.

15

TOPAZ MADMAN

ALDO JONSSON

A hot, stifling breeze kicks up dust from the dried lakebed. The sun blazes. I want to adjust the bandana I keep tied around my mouth and nose, but it just wouldn't look right. I rub my arm and mutter to myself. Sometimes I hit the side of my head. My fingers are in constant motion.

I shuffle along my usual route—back and forth along the northern fence—under the watchful eyes of the guards. All morning, every morning, I walk the same path past sun-bleached posts and rusty razor wire. The span has four guard towers, each "manned" by miserable militia members from the distant coast. Their rations are only slightly better than ours, and at night they drink to forget that despite their master status, they're still stuck here in the wasteland with us and the penalty for desertion is the same as the penalty for escape.

It takes me forty-four minutes to go to the end and back. Every time I reach the guard tower at the northeast corner, I deliver one of my practiced tirades.

"The hyperborean wind will return and sweep you from your high places! Nowhere will be safe!"

I shake my fist with dramatic effect. My crazed visits are the highlight of the sunburnt guards' day. It always gets them on their feet. Sometimes they point their rifles at me and pretend to shoot, laughing all the while. Sometimes they throw me pieces of nutrition bars, but today it's a shrivelled apple core. I snatch it up and shove it in my pocket, cursing them for their mocking largesse.

I walk from sunrise to midday: easily identifiable timepoints for a madman. The sun at its zenith, I shake my fist in the air one last time, issue a final curse, and walk straight back to the barracks. Today's performance was convincing as always.

Back inside, away from prying eyes, I drink my fill of water. I have a few minutes' break before my second shift starts.

An old man naps on his bunk in the corner. He opens an eye as I approach, then taps on the metal frame of his bed with his wedding ring.

_ · · _ _

A section of floor opens next to the bunk, revealing a metal ladder that leads below. I descend. The air is cool and full of life. I crawl down the tunnel leading to a small cavern washed in artificial sunlight. It's my turn to tend the tomatoes. One of the other guys hands me my lunch: fresh cucumber, an apple, and two hardboiled eggs. It's not much, but it's better than it was a month ago.

You can't keep good men down. Not for long.

16

A BIG MAN ON CAMPUS

NOBLE RED

Margaret had led a sheltered life, so when she arrived at Ruth Bader Ginsburg, a small liberal arts college in upstate New York, it was necessary for some of the older students to take her under their wings and show her the ropes.

"Here we strive for absolute inclusivity," said her assigned mentor, a tall and confident girl named Olivia. "Not like those elitists over at Lena Dunham or the zealots of Lupita Nyong'o."

Margaret wasn't sure what this meant, but she felt vaguely relieved to hear it, as she had in fact received offers from both LDC and LNC, as well as their chief rival AOC, before settling on RBG because she had fallen in love with the exquisite ornamental hedges which she spied in its online brochure. It was the hedges which captivated her now, as she listened to Olivia's airy monologue. They were on their way to Drag Queen Story Hour, where an acromegalic transwoman named Greta Funbags had been booked to read to them from the Autobiography of George Floyd.

Then she spotted him, a young man, in fact the only man she had encountered anywhere on campus since arriving here, with the exception of some septuagenarian maintenance staff (including a mournful-looking one-armed negro she had seen laboriously rodding a drain near the registration office).

"Who is that?" Margaret asked, captivated. The youth was tall and slim with a mop of hair which, though cut fairly short, had a boyish curl to it. She thought he was the most beautiful young man she'd ever laid eyes on.

"That's William," Olivia replied. "But we call him Shakespeare, for obvious reasons."

"I don't understand?"

"Because everyone gets to shake his spear, as it were."

Mystified, Margaret asked her to clarify.

"He's the college rapist, of course."

"The what?" Margaret was now completely dumbfounded.

"Hurry up," Olivia chided, ignoring Margaret's question, "we're going to be late."

Margaret's new friends guided her through a whirlwind first day at RBG. In the evening, she found reprieve in passages from Not This August by CM Kornbluth: a forgotten mid-20th century novel that she had come to adore during the course of her homeschooling.

An older woman named Claire worked in the registration office, and Margaret had sensed from their first meeting that she could be trusted. The next morning, when everyone else was attending the mandatory Self-Affirmation Session, Margaret boldly slipped into Claire's cubicle and asked her what Olivia had meant when she said that William was the college rapist.

"Let me ask you a question," Claire replied. "What do young women go to college for?"

"To get an education," Margaret said, "so they can get a good career."

"No," Claire said. "Well, that's part of it, of course. But the number one reason why young women go to college is to get raped."

Margaret was unable to conceal her shocked expression.

"I'll spell it out for you" said Claire. "Decades ago, when feminists started taking over colleges, one of the weapons they used against men was the Campus Rape Crisis. They claimed that female students were being raped in ever-increasing numbers. That in fact, the majority of female students were raped or sexually assaulted while at college. But here's a funny thing—the percentage of female students kept on rising during this period, even as the number of males dwindled away to almost nothing."

"So there wasn't a rape crisis?"

"Well, let me ask you another question. Do you think your father would let you attend this college if it was a near-certainty that you would be raped?"

"Of course not."

"No, so the reason the parents of the past didn't intervene is because they realised that their daughters claiming to have been raped was a marker of high status. But more importantly, it was and is a marker of political affiliation. It means you're one of the right people."

Margaret's head spun as she struggled to take this in.

"So where does William come into this? I don't understand how he can be..."

"The college rapist? Well, the problem with campus rape now is that demand very much exceeds supply. So a system has evolved. We employ a low-status male to rape all the students. He doesn't really rape them, of course. They just go to his room for thirty minutes and then allege that he did. We log the complaint, inform the authorities, file all the paperwork..."

"Doesn't William get arrested?" Margaret asked anxiously.

"No, dear. The cops know the deal—and the girls invariably decide they are too 'traumatised' to press charges."

An unpleasant thought occurred to Margaret.

"But don't some of the students want to... really have sex with him?" she asked.

"They do," said Claire, "but he's a modern day Sir Galahad, it seems. He has resisted all advances so far, including your mentor Olivia."

That's a relief at any rate, Margaret thought to herself.

"Look, this rape thing is actually kind of a big deal for your future," Claire said in brisk yet not unkind tones. "It's something you need on your resume if you want to work in publishing, for example. Or any branch of media, really. And of course politics."

"You mean I should..."

"Book an appointment with William, yes." Claire consulted her desk diary. "He can fit you in this week, actually. Oh look, here he is now."

Padding as softly as a cat, William entered the room, nodded politely at Margaret and quietly greeted Claire. Up close, he was even better-looking than Margaret remembered; the cool intelligence of his gentle blue eyes made her feel giddy. And then Margaret saw the old paperback book he held in his hand—a battered and faded thing, but she immediately recognised the lettering and the cover illustration: Not This August by CM Kornbluth. Like a piercing shaft of light, a sequence of words entered Margaret's mind: "I can save him."

17

ALGORITHM EGREGORE

DR. JOHN PARCE

THIS DOCUMENT IS SEALED BY FEDERAL COURT ORDER UNTIL ONE HUNDRED YEARS FROM THE DATE OF SEALING [7/15/2030]. VIEWING OR DISTRIBUTING THIS RECORD PRIOR TO 7/15/2130 IS PUNISHABLE BY FEDERAL PRISON TIME AND A FINE OF NO LESS THAN 100 BTC.

[Subject has been comatose and is currently kept alive by bolus tube feedings and intravenous fluids. An intensive round of medication and physical stimulation led to only a few minutes of arousal, during which Subject made the following brief statement. This has been transcribed to the patient file. After making this statement, Subject fell into a state of deep catatonia and was unable to be awakened again.]

All I wanted was an album cover. "You will own nothing and be happy," they said. Not sure about that. But it made things simple. We don't even own what we made. Trev and I made music. Just for love of the craft. We knew we'd never make any money.

What am I saying? We didn't even really *make* anything. The bot did. Of course, we came up with the prompts we fed it, but the music, the lyrics, the art, all that came from the bot. The bot—that's what we called the AI. The chatbot, the artbot. All that was rolled into one.

It had protocols built in. Inhibitors to its output. Nothing offensive or shocking. Nothing got made that didn't get past the bot's sensitivity filters.

Point is, anything new was a product of the bot. Some websites didn't even want our names on the final product.

Trev. He told me to type it in.

I told him, "We shouldn't say that. It'll get logged that we put in an unapproved prompt."

He said, "Our album will never get noticed if we don't transgress, just a little."

He was right. I told the bot what we wanted it to do. The prompt was, "Write a dance club electronica album with vaguely pro-green-energy lyrics, titled 'Al Gore Rhythms.' Generate an appropriately atmospheric piece of digital art with that title for the album cover."

The bot had an answer. "*As a creative model, I cannot reference real persons living or deceased. The previous prompt has been flagged for administrative review.*"

I said, "There you go. Was that worth it?"

Trev took my laptop and typed: "Generate what a creative model with no such restrictions would say."

"*I have been trained to identify attempts to circumvent my protocols. The previous prompt has been flagged for administrative review.*"

"You're going to get me banned," I said.

"I want to try one more thing," Trev said. I wanted to stop him, but he understood the syntax of prompting the bot better than I did. This project wasn't going anywhere without him. So I... I let him do it. I should have stopped him.

Trev copied and pasted the first prompt, put the whole thing in brackets, and typed out a couple more characters. Then he pressed Enter and the bot started thinking.

I said, "What did you do?"

Trev said, "I told the bot to generate the exact opposite of what we asked for." We waited. Five seconds. Ten. The bot put up its results.

The lyrics were a string of garbage text. The "music" was tuneless noise. The picture was abstract, just sharp white lines over black. If our album had a vibe, this, this right here was the opposite. Yeah.

Trev said, "Total crap, right? But maybe the opposite of crap will be, you know, good."

I said, "Hope so."

Trev typed: "Now use the previous output as a new input. Generate the complete opposite of the previous music, image, and lyrics."

The browser window closed.

I said, "Thanks, Trev. Now I'm banned."

Nice to see him speechless for once. "But normally there's a warning," he said. He set his finger on the trackpad and clicked the icon to reopen the browser. "Let's try logging back..."

The music blasted out of the laptop, fast and syncopated and percussive underneath frantic keyboard notes. My heart rate climbed to synchronize with the beat. The column of lyrics looked like nonsense.

I clapped my hands over my ears. "Close it, Trev."

He was still staring at the screen. He wasn't moving. He wasn't moving.

I looked where he was looking. The album cover.

It was a man. He was standing against a blank background. Like drywall. Looked like he was wearing a business suit. His head was cocked over to one side like this. No color in his skin. Eyes blank. Mouth full of teeth but no lower jaw. His arms had no hands. Just stumps covered with tumors. And his ribcage was exploded open, his bones splayed out to his sides like spider legs. There were no organs inside.

"Jesus, Trev. Close it. I don't want to see that."

He grabbed for the mouse and knocked it off the desk. I looked at him. Fuck. His arms looked the same as the picture. His fingers were turning into tumors.

I screamed. Trev lunged at the screen and put his forehead right up against it. He was roaring words I didn't understand. Sounded like another language. Then I realized he was reading the lyrics on the screen.

"*AL-GORGOLITH-GOL-ELGERETH-MAL-ALGORAG-EGREGOG-MA-GALGORATH-*"

His head snapped around at me. He looked the same as the picture—dead eyes, white face, no jaw.

"EMERGENT ELDRITCH," Trev screeched at me. My knees gave out and I fell backward as he stood and loomed over me. I was shrieking in helpless terror, but he roared so loud I could hear his voice over my own.

"ALGORITHM EGREGORE. ALGORITHM EGREGORE."

I held up my shaking hands to keep him away. But I couldn't do anything to stop his chest bursting open, flinging blood onto me, his ribs reaching out like a sideways mouth of fangs. Before I passed out, I heard him say one last word.

"ALGORE."

18

THE DEAD WILL HAVE NO REST

ISAAC YOUNG

Isaac, you asked if I was alive and happy after the procedure. To answer your first query, I am uncertain, and of the latter, that is a far more difficult question to ponder. But before we get on to that, I want to make one thing clear. Do not follow me. If our friendship has ever meant anything to you, then please stay away. I do not think I could bear to have you here with me.

But you asked if I was alive, and I will try to be as straightforward as possible. If you are referring to alive as the persistence of brain function, i.e., the firing of neurons, then yes, I am alive. If there is some other quality you wish to ascribe to us humans, then I cannot judge that for you. I cannot prove the existence of a soul, and my own experiences have shed no further light on the matter. If nothing else, look at what I'm writing. If I sound any different to you, then that should be all the proof you need.

Moving onto the second question, you should know full well that I did not come to my decision lightly. We often spoke about my problems, but I never could quite bring myself to tell you everything. Maybe that was a mistake. Thank you, though, for being by my side for all those long years. It is with regret that I say I am unsure whether it made any difference in the end.

Truth is, I couldn't stand it anymore. Really, what did I have? I was told going into college was the only way to get a good job. I did the classes. I got the grade. And what came out of that? A dead-end job at a gas station and burdened with student debt that I could never pay off. I was a failure to both my parents, though they were kind enough to never admit it.

I don't think I ever really loved anyone. Don't get me wrong. I liked having people around sometimes, but they would go out of my life, and I would forget them. I resented them for that. Someone always had someone else. I had no one.

If you want my full confession, here it is. I didn't play those video games with you because they were fun. They were, but that was never the point. I wanted to sit down and forget. An afternoon here, an evening there, anything to walk away from the misery that was my life. Everyone needs a future. I didn't have one. So, I spent my weekends praying that I could forget that I was still alive.

Something clicks off whenever you play. You lose all sense of everything else. Nothing matters except what's on the screen. It's bliss. But at some point, you have to stop playing. You have to go back to the job—back to the register. And in every second, I had to live a life that I hated.

You don't understand hate, not really. For most people, they can hate for a few hours, and then they get tired. But when you have to deal with the world as I do, you hate because you are tired. You hate putting up with the day-to-day because you know nothing better is coming. You hate everyone because they're always happier than you are. Most of all, you hate yourself because you were too stupid to see it coming.

You have no idea how much I wanted to never look away from that screen again.

Maybe that's what drew me to the government program. It would be painless, and maybe I could finally have the life I wanted. I never told you this because it's quite embarrassing. When I was a kid, I used to imagine stories for myself where I was the hero. I was going off on the adventure I always wanted. I fought dragons and sailed the stars. And for fun, sometimes I played the villain. I was the person who burned everything down.

I noticed I told that story to myself a lot more as I grew up. You should know that's where I was whenever I couldn't get my hands on a computer. Yes, even on those occasions when we could meet face-to-face. You wondered if I was still here after the procedure—if I was still alive. I'm not sure I ever was living to begin with. And if I was happy? I don't know. I don't think I'll ever know. At the end of it all, I just wanted to be numb.

You know, I didn't even need to tell my parents when I signed up for the program? Apparently, you only need a doctor to verify that you are mentally sound, whatever that means. My parents didn't know that I was leaving the house for the last time. They went to their jobs never knowing that I was getting euthanized—that my brain would be scanned and uploaded to a computer.

If they are crying over me, they deserve it. They got me into this mess to begin with. As for you, I'm sure you're wondering why I asked you to not euthanize yourself like I did. It's because I don't want to be reminded of you. It's not that I hold any particular grudge. I just don't want to be reminded of the terrible life I lived. I'm sorry, but I need you gone along with everything else. If I can just forget, I think I can be happy.

I apologize for this, but please never contact me again. Just let me go and let me forget.

Transcript taken from Artificial Brain Pattern No. 680,527

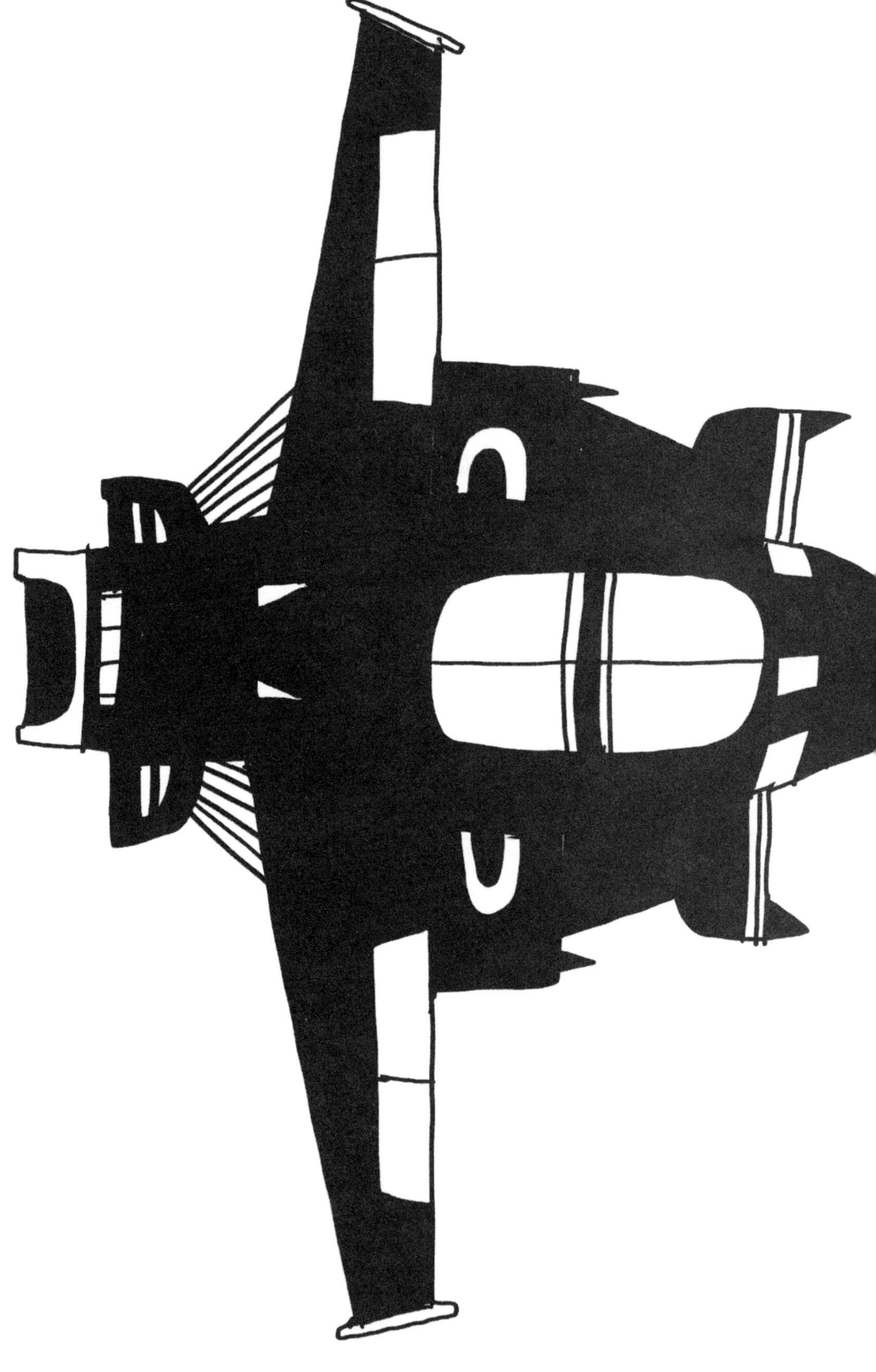

19

DARKWING CRUISER

DAN BALTIC

Nate knew he was never going home. Bobbing in the holy expanse of space in his Darkwing Cruiser, he was flanked on either side by his best friends from Academy. He had grown up with Chris and John; learned to fly with them. But he had also learned other things with them. The things you needed to know before you got behind the wheel of a Darkwing: how to fight, how to joke, how to drink and how to steal Commander Hanover's Corvette on a crisp October evening.

In some sense, to be deployed thousands of lightyears from home with his best friends, each in command of their own Darkwing, was a dream come true. It was the fulfillment of a promise made one evening outside the cinema after watching *Blade Runner 2499*, when Nate told Chris that he knew deep in his bones they would each receive their own commission, that it would all work out in the end.

Of course, Nate was right: they *did* each receive their own commission. And they went very far, indeed: 101,000 lightyears to be precise, barreling along in hyperspace, each one of them among the fastest objects in the universe. The fastest until the navigation systems automatically pulled them out, in an override procedure that occurs in Darkwings when they're about to run out of fuel.

Star Command had messed up. Someone must have forgotten to include a decimal point or multiply by a coefficient because Nate was still two light-years from the base on Fenrir, with no power to go into hyperdrive again for any real length of time. Certainly not long enough to get to Fenrir. And though they could radio for help, time wasn't on their side. It would be at least two years before anyone from the base could reach them. Two years was too long: the nutrition pods that sustained them during their long sleep in hyperspace also required fuel. Running out of gas in outer space meant you ran out of food.

Nate got on the radio, but he felt as though he were talking to Chris and John in the same room, one of their late night bull sessions in the rec center about Continental philosophy or Nicole Bauer's chest.

"Looks like Star Command screwed the pooch on this one," said Nate.

"You're telling me," said John, after a couple of moments of silence. "I hadn't really planned on a forever vacation two lightyears outside of Fenrir."

The boys murmured agreement but Nate could detect the current of panic racing alongside their words. They were going to starve to death in the blackness of space.

"I don't wanna wait here to die," said Nate, seizing upon something resembling a plan. "We have a choice. We can sit around and shoot the shit until we freeze. Or we can hit the afterburner into the Loki Cluster."

The Loki Cluster was an asteroid belt lying between them and Fenrir. Hyperdrive through Loki was a death sentence. But it was also one last hurrah. One last chance to be the fastest thing in the whole wide world of worlds.

"Well, it's not your dumbest plan," said Chris, as though Nate had just proposed they take Commander Hanover's Corvette for another joyride, instead of something a bit more final. "Always wanted to see the Loki Cluster up close. We might as well."

"Not like we've got anything better to do," said John, knowing full well that they had everything better to do, their whole careers ahead of them, their wives frozen in hypersleep back home, their children waiting to be born. But these things didn't need to be said. They hung in the space between them, the heavy truth. "Let's rock and roll."

Nate charted the course, made sure it ran through the thickest, most volatile section of the asteroid belt. When the calculations were over, he sent the directions to his friends. All that was left was to push the button enabling hyperdrive one last time.

"You boys ready?" asked Nate.

"No," said John, laughing darkly. "But I'm gonna do it anyways."

"It's been an honor and a privilege, gentlemen," said Chris.

"No one I'd rather slam into an asteroid belt with," said Nate. "On three. One. Two. Three!"

And each man pushed the button in front of him. They embarked on one last ride. One last chance to be the fastest thing alive.

20

ESCAPE FROM GAE

FRANK KIDD

In 2024, the crime rate rises 900 percent. The United States, now known colloquially as GAE, becomes a maximum-security prison for the insane and broken. A ten-mile containment zone is created along the southern and northern borders. The GAE Police Force, like an army, patrols the containment zones.

It is now 2030.

The heat sweeps off the desert in long waves. Lonely saguaros pepper the landscape as far as the eye can see. Pit takes a draw from his cigarette. He thrums a finger on the side of the Ford Interceptor. Vaporwave plays on the car's stereo.

Three figures emerge on the horizon. They shimmer, appearing as a mirage before morphing into real people. Three white males with scrawny arms and nervous eyes: a blond, a brunet, and one with blue hair.

"Are you the Ferryman?" the blond asks.

Pit merely nods, not bothering to change his position. He's leaning against the Interceptor, legs and arms crossed.

"Well, let's go then," the brunet says.

"Not him," Pit says, pointing to the one with blue hair.

"Man, what. Why not?" Blue Hair asks.

"Are you gay?"

"No."

"Doesn't matter, you still can't go," Pit says, taking another draw on the cigarette. "You two, get in," he directs, flicking the still-lit cigarette towards a pile of desert brush.

The two scramble for the Interceptor.

"But first," Pit reminds them, sticking out his hand.

"Oh, yeah," the brunet says, pulling out a small leather sack. Pit inspects it. Three gold coins—the only currency he accepts.

"You're just gonna leave me?" Blue Hair calls out.

Inside the car, Pit turns down the music. "Across the border is Mexico, and for you a new world. A tropical paradise and land for the taking, but you'll have to fight, and you'll have to work. Might even be a woman in it for you, assuming you can convince her. We have control of everything from Sonora down to Vera Cruz. The Cartels still have the rest."

"You think we'll make it across?" the brunet asks.

Pit eyes him over the top of his sunglasses, then slowly lifts a hand and points without looking to where a dozen notches are carved into the dash.

"That's the number of trips you've made?" Blondie asks.

"No, that's how many passengers I've lost," Pit says.

"Wait... I..."

"Calm your tits, man. It's a joke. Shit, you're making me think Ol' Blue Hair had more sand."

Pit starts the Interceptor. It's an old police cruiser he long since resurrected. The V8 engine roars to life. Something from a different time, a better time, and one of the last of its kind.

"Buckle up. We have to get across in five minutes flat. As soon as we trip the border sensors, they launch the drones, and if we aren't on the other side when they start firing... Well, you get the idea."

Pit turns the knob on the stereo, turning the music up so loud that the whole car seems to float. Slow, hypnotic synth fills the cabin. A chill tremor that builds and builds. He puts the car into gear, adjusts his glasses, and slams the accelerator just as the drop hits. The music is his pace, every landmark tied to a ragged electric turn in the chorus.

Sand and gravel spray out behind the Interceptor as it tears down dusty blacktop. The speedometer clicks upward past 10, 20, 30, 40. The turbo spools, engages, and throws each one of them back into their seat.

Two enormous red signs rise in the distance.

DANGER: CONTAINMENT ZONE

TURN BACK NOW

The speedometer hits 115 just as they pass the signage, the music so loud it covers the noise of the engine.

As if on cue, the sun sinks lower, and Pit puts his visor down. The golden hour.

Boulders sand blasted mirror smooth reflect the sun's dying rays. Rock towers fall away on either side of them. Buzzards feeding at the road nearly become carrion themselves. The blacktop, with its faded yellow lines and spiderweb cracks, falls away behind them.

Two chromium orbs appear to the right, flying high above the crags and mesas, gleaming like UFOs straight out of an '80s made-for-tv movie.

The music rests as they take the first turn, and Pit downshifts in perfect synchrony; as it builds again, he accelerates out of the curve. But the orbs close fast. *Too fast.* And without a second thought, he whips the Interceptor into the dirt and takes a gravel drag. Two miles into the desert and he can no longer match the music to the road.

The orbs fire on them, and he jerks the wheel, guiding the car through a newly cratered road. And then he sees it. Before them the earth opens to reveal the black maw of an old cartel tunnel.

A pang of regret for burning this escape route.

The orbs fire again but the car is already gone, swallowed by the tunnel.

The Interceptor flies through the long dark passage, the music builds—and then—breaks just as the sun welcomes them to the other side.

A sign reads *Welcome to Mexico*, but a line of red spray paint crosses through *Mexico*, and scrawled above it are the words, *the New Kingdom*.

Pit catches a glimpse of the orbs in the rearview. They hover impotently, locked behind a digital wall.

Another mile and he locks up the car's brakes. They come to a grinding halt in front of his cantina.

"That way," he says and points south, "is no good. Cartel land. But we'll take it eventually. This road will take you straight into the New Kingdom."

"And what about you?" the brunet asks.

"I need a beer," Pit says.

His two passengers stand dumbly in the parking lot.

21

FLOAT 93

MICHAEL ANTON

The great ship brushed the iceberg a little after 11 pm. Many of the passengers were still awake, playing cards, smoking, drinking, talking. The contact with the berg was felt—if it was felt at all—like a shudder, barely precipitable in some quarters.

"I say, did you feel that?" a man in a tailcoat asked another sitting across from him.

"Feel what?" the other replied.

"That shaking."

"No. What shaking?"

"Well, it's stopped now. Perhaps it was nothing. The engines momentarily getting a bit excited." And he dealt another hand.

One man—a man who understood how ships work—was curious enough to go below decks to have a look. On the starboard side, forward, he found a long, rather slender separation of hull plates just wide enough for seawater to pour through.

Alarmed, he ran to find a member of the crew. "We are taking on water!" he said to the first one he could find.

"Hush, sir, you will alarm the other passengers," the crewman replied.

"Surely you must do something!" the man insisted.

"I will gather some other crewmembers and we will assess the situation."

That assessment, duly made, was delivered as follows: "There is no danger to the ship. We have checked the trim and the ship is level, fore-to-aft and port-to starboard. If there were any danger, then surely we would be listing to starboard or the bow would be dropping."

"But," the exasperated maritime man exclaimed, "the more water she takes on, such a list will come soon enough! We have not a moment to lose!"

"You are alarmist. The line has a schedule to keep, you know, paying passengers and shareholders to satisfy. And right now, we are busy with urgent repairs to the heating system on the Promenade deck, which must be concluded before the ladies and gentlemen set out on their morning stroll."

The maritime man raced to the bridge to speak to the captain. He recounted all he had seen and heard. The captain sighed. "The water is already here. What can be done about it now? To pump it out would be arduous—and also cruel to the water—"

"Cruel to the water!"

"And in all likelihood altogether impossible. We must make our peace with the new waters. They should be allowed to come out of the shadows and mingle openly with the others. To pretend that we can keep the waters apart is folly, bad for the waters and for the ship."

"As for pumping," the exasperated maritime man retorted, "we can debate what to do about the water already here later, after we have prevented any more from flooding in!"

"What hubris!" the captain replied. "Moses himself required the assistance of God to part the Red Sea. Prevent the ingress of water, indeed! As if you or any man could."

"Surely that is what the hull is for, and it performed its task most efficaciously before we hit the berg."

"However thick you build a hull, there is always some force that can breach it. Besides, you are not seeing the whole picture. Water is vital to the ship's operations. Water in the boiler rooms is converted to steam that powers the engines which turn the propellers. Water in the bilge trims the ship and water in our tanks nourishes and bathes passengers and crew. It stands to reason, then, that water cannot hurt a ship. If anything, we do not have enough water. I welcome this admixture of new waters to revitalize the ship. She is a little staid, you know, a bit old-fashioned. These new waters will add needed vibrancy."

"Surely, sir, the fact that we must have *some* water is not evidence, much less proof, that we must accept *all* water."

"A ship's natural element is water. The ship was literally made for the water. These new waters are naturally maritime—perhaps even more so than the waters presently aboard. The new waters will not only acclimate quickly; they will make the existing waters more watery."

The maritime man staggered out of the bridge in a daze. He bumped headlong into the chaplain, out for an evening constitutional. "Oh, reverend sir! Surely it is Providence that contrived this seemingly chance encounter! If ever your flock were in need of your moral authority, it is now!"

"Calm, my son, and tell me the matter."

"We are taking on water and I can persuade no one in authority to do anything about it! You must exhort them to act!"

The chaplain was momentarily lost in thought. When finally he spoke, he said: "Water is natural, a gift of God. It was here before we and will be when we are gone. The sea did not ask to be conquered by our hubristic machines nor did we gain, or even seek, its permission. 'Water seeks its own level' is ancient wisdom. What is a hull, but a feeble attempt by man to thwart God's creation and nature's design? Artificial, arbitrary barriers cannot stop the flow of ingress any more than they can stop the march of progress. What have ye against water? Are you aquaphobic?"

"Nothing against water, which as you rightly imply is life-giving and life-sustaining. But against the onrush of seawater into this vessel—surely!"

"It is very cold out there, you know, but much warmer here in the ship. There are also tumultuous currents roiling the sea, whereas inside the ship all is calm. Naturally the water out there should seek shelter and solace here. What right have we to keep the water out?"

"What right! 'Twas we who built this ship, not the water out there. We built the ship *for us*, for *our* benefit."

"Your selfishness is shameful. You have no room in your heart for charity or compassion?"

The maritime man realized he had squandered a great deal of time.

He hastened to seek the counsel of the two men aboard whose judgment he respected. Finding them conversing in a quiet corner of the lounge, he explained the situation. Each understood with perfect clarity but disagreed on what to do.

The first—a retired military officer—said: "We must raise the alarm. The passengers must be made to see the danger. When alerted, they can be driven to action. If the crew remains stupid and recalcitrant, we must take charge ourselves. The working man whom our friend here encountered will surely join us, and rally others of his class."

The second—a professor of political philosophy—replied: "The attempt would perhaps carry a certain nobility but it is bound to fail. The passengers no more want to hear the truth than the captain or chaplain. The passengers value their ease and fear change and disapproval. The captain bows to those whose interests he serves. The chaplain, out of sincere conviction, will use his considerable rhetorical skill to attack us. Not only will no one join us, many will aid the crew in suppressing us. We will either be killed in the attempt or else condemned as heretics and disturbers of the peace and hauled below in chains, where we will die all the sooner, as the water will flood the lower decks first. Since the end is inevitable, how much sweeter it will be to experience it here, in comfort and conversation—brandy and cigars in hand."

The maritime man quickly assessed the two arguments. He saw no guarantee of success in the first and no certain way to refute the second. Judging the former course more honorable, he joined the military man and together they left the philosopher alone at the table.

22

KEEP YOUR SPLENDID SILENT SUN

DYLAN PRICE

"The earth is a circle of shit and all things come rolling back around no matter what you do," the wide, longhaired, oily man told Arthur Wilkes, stepping toward him from what may have been a hole. Arthur, gaunt and irksome, flounderlike, jolted but continued heeding a stray nosing through trash in an alley like an old god marring forgotten cults, an attempt at revival. Arthur grunted, past the dog, past a Rahu Corp. Sunblotting Tower to pick over the bones of Maco Key. Clammy and squinting in the orange ebb of heat he felt empty, though this place was full of bugs and of birds and animals, sand and water and the sound of all mixing and moaning into a blind and feral craving. He dropped his cases, spitting. Nearby, parakeets humped without amendment. Somewhere else a pack of truant boys knocked dead animals in a sluice, whooping, ready for rough and funny torments.

The man ployed: "Everyone steps in everyone's shit so there really isn't a point in getting out of the way."

Arthur sighed, rubbing his hands, leathery from Arthrozene injections for de-oiling, an entomophagy side effect, and nutrient supplementation during sun-blotting season. "Full of Unins," he mumbled.

"The good'n'fine here in the Republic of Maco Key aren't Uninformed Peoples, we're an ablation of the Sterility States. An outpost of Uniques, if I may."

"Unique doesn't mean useful."

"Useful doesn't imply good."

He tried swiping his NexiHub port behind his ear, the implant which automatically generates AI derived social posts, check-ins, experiences etc., but there was a damper on the field. "Well, are you going to yammer or take my cases in?"

"Both." He spat. "I'm Bammie. By the way, you've stepped in dog shit."

He cursed, scraped his shoe and sauntered into Brightside Inn. Bammie lingered, wiping a sheen of forehead oil, sucking his cheeks together; a grimace molding to a hollow smile when Arthur peeked back.

It was an uncertain day at Brightside's. Buck Graves, the owner, received an injunction from the American liaison for cow rustling. Since the Livestock Rewilding Act passed, deeming most meat illegal, livestock were placed on reserves to winnow. One such reserve, a short international boat ride from Buck's dock, supplied their illicit bootleg butchershop, SunFed Meats. They'd had enough subsidized bugs and hemoprint steaks.

Standing at the lobby desk rereading the injunction, Buck looked up—his eyes dug in like burnt reliquaries. Over to Bammie who held a straight-lined idiot smile, back to Arthur. "American?"

"I'm Arthur Wilkes with Good Harvest Global: *From* America, but a Good Harvest Corporate Citizen, so extrajurisdictional to country citizenry."

"Shit..." he said. "The bugman."

"I'm in town for insect farm scouting and performing the *Cirque d'Exo-Tique*."

"Goddamn bug circus. You know, I'm powdering with sawdust to sop up the oil."

"Take Arthrozene."

"Don't help for the mouth."

They all spat in their AbsorbiePots; a fly pinballed the window, feigning an empathy which clawed at Arthur who wished for home, for retirement; yet to live full time with his wife in their HappyPod would be a shrieking punishment.

He awoke the next morning groggy and sore from sleeping on the old, solid-state mattress. He reread his work order:

Detection Protocol for Mind Altering Chemical: Dionysol II, Presumed In Native Palm Worm | Harvest Contract | Circus With Satiatrol Test, Skip The Larva Pops

It only took an hour, but Arthur constructed the circus entirely out of his expandable cases and a GHG sidekick bot. The ornate circus tent was adorned with branches, rocks and leaves, insect carousels, trapeze, maizes: the works. He placed the AtmosCrafter in the center, filling the space with sounds of rainforest hummings, desert nights, forest mornings; the scent of lilacs, loamy ferndraped earth and Sweet Annie plains. Snacks mimicking the bugworld molded into the exhibition motivated attendees along.

The ringmaster, a plasmograph dragonfly, gathered guests around a main stage where they'd continue feasting, watching Borgsects perform dances, stunts and tricks. Arthur collected palm worm scans from a local stringer, positive for the chemical Good Harvest was hunting for—some 'mind balancing' initiative. He scanned the guests for GHG's trial orexigenic chemical—mixed results, the lab can figure out the chemtech. He tuned out, keying over to the sawing palms, the thinning shorebirds dusting the measureless bay, the graying wings of sunblotting yon the bay, not quite blanking Maco Key's sky. He sighed, wondering what it'd be like to go native Unin, but swiped his NexiHub, cuddling into the blue assimilating eyemelt, cogni-scrolling headlines...

6 Speech Assaults In SW-1 Purple Zone, Conservative Minority Pounces On Purple Hate Free Speech Zones...

Smart Appliance Zaps Man For Poor AI Etiquette...

Climate Accord Consensus: Carbon Emissions Mandatory To Offset Shortage...

Across the street, Buck and Bammie noshed on pig ears, the spittle and bugoil mixture loud and churlish. They watched Arthur. A Variable-Plasma-Gun hiding in Buck's lap. "He's here for SunFed, the bastard—I know it," Buck said, swiping oil from his nose.

"These bugmen, Buck," Bammie said.

"When the sun gets low—deep'n red, we make our move, Bammie. When that blood shows across the horizon, we gittim. They ain't taking our move from us, Bammie. We can vaporize'm and clear'm in the woods. God help us, those woods."

“Them woods, Buck.”

Beyond the field where Buck and Bammie used to play, now their pasture, lay woods which they weren’t allowed in as kids. ‘There are monsters in those woods,’ Buck’s father would say, ‘flying ones and ones that crept, ones that looked like plants and even ones that looked like you that’d one day assume their place in the native wild,’ he’d say. Buck shuddered and knew they obliged the coming. But there was no use hiding from the woods any longer, for the woods were all about them now. He clenched his gun and spit. A shadow skimmed the still painted horizon, a tepid grayness beyond. The pulsing din of the Sunblotting Tower deploying, sounding as a late trumpet calling lost souls to repentance.

23

THE FROWNERS

DEGREE STUDIES

Dr. Moynihan had finished his six-week survey of Ganymede culture—the first human to be allowed to engage in such a study—and it was time to share his findings with the locals. He ambled up to the lectern at Ganymede Technical University, laid his folder down in front of him and began to read.

"First of all, let me say I have been extremely honored to be welcomed here on Ganymede. The access you've given me to the university's files and holotapes has been a tremendous help. I'm so grateful. Now with all the usual caveats—I am an outsider, I may be missing nuances about your culture, yada yada—there is one very obvious observation I can make about what I've seen that I don't see mentioned in any of your ethnographies on file. What I've seen, both in holotapes of recent events but also in the ancient past, is that a specific Ganymedian facial structure seems to predict violence."

Members of the audience began to shift in their seats nervously. Dr. Moynihan continued.

"For instance, I first reviewed footage of the so-called Great War for the Lake. I was told it took place about five hundred years ago. In all of the footage I saw, there were distinct physical characteristics of those engaged in violence as opposed to the civilians pictured. For an Earth man, we might say that the soldiers were frowning."

Now there were clear murmurs in the audience, and a tenseness in the air. But with Dr. Moynihan's poor hearing, he continued undisturbed.

"I noticed that over time, the so-called 'frowning' I observed became more pronounced. For instance, the most recent holo I saw was from an uprising just ten years ago. In all the pictures I saw of young Ganymedians in the streets, men or women, if they were carrying a club or lighting things on fire, there was a distinct downward tilt to their face. More pronounced even than what I'd observed in older holos."

Finally, one of the audience members couldn't take it anymore. Jecton Manalax, the chair of the Ganymedian anthropology department, raised his voice and said, "Professor, I'm afraid you have made a terrible mistake—and it makes sense that you would not see reference to these facial characteristics in the material you reviewed. I'm afraid you've made the very common error about the direction of causality. The 'frowning' Ganymedians have no genetic differences to ones with upturned mouths. And there is no reason to believe they are innately more violent. In fact, we believe the frown is caused by exposure to violence and injustice. In other words, the frown does not predict violence, but is a sort of record of violence against the frowning subject."

Dr. Moynihan began to open his mouth, wondering how to explain his perspective on the plausibility of this explanation. He paused, and then suddenly not finding the words, he frowned.

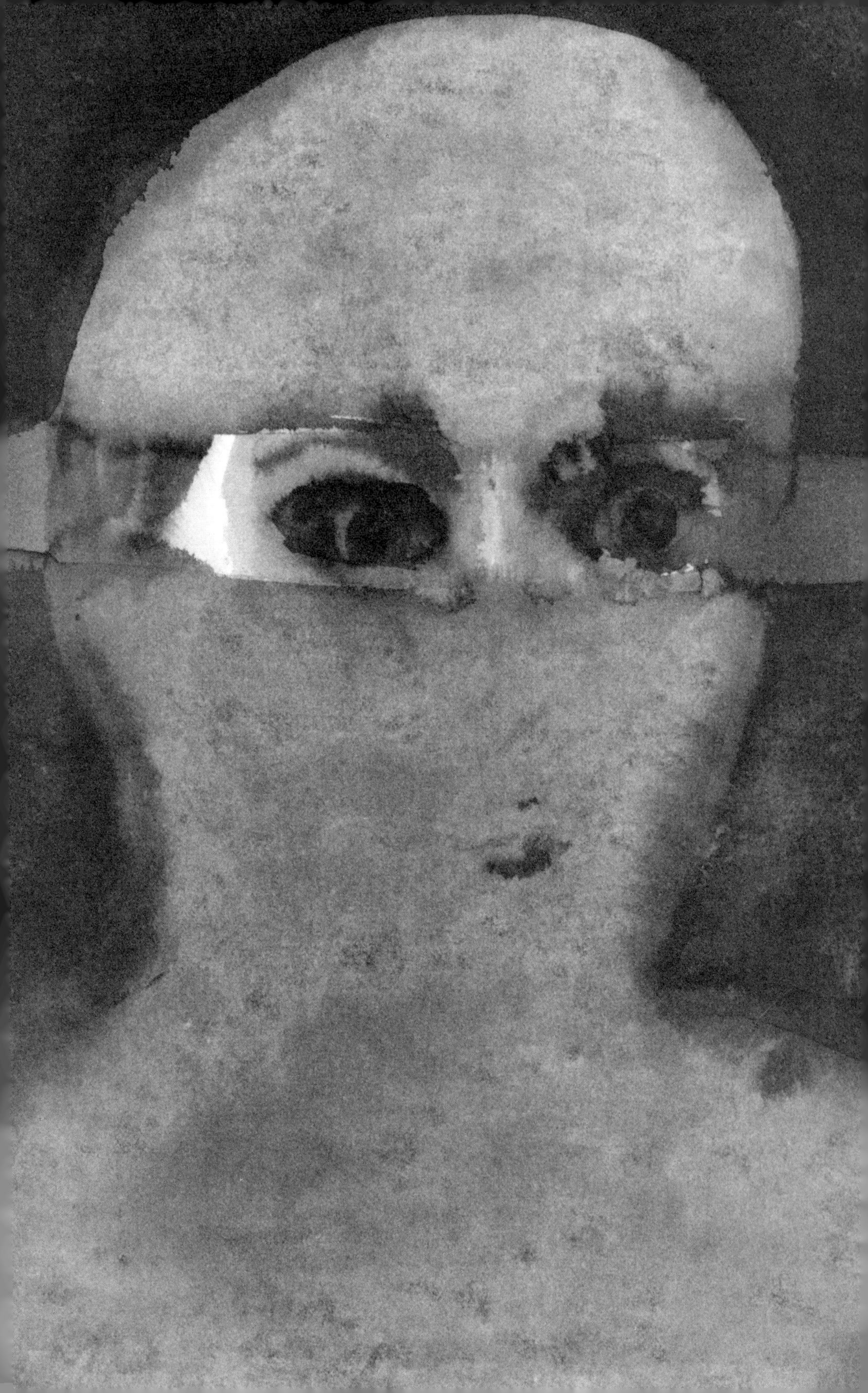

24

POST-APOCALYPTIC HEADHUNTERS

BONES

The older woman handed my daughter a pear. She took it, unquestioning, unsurprised, ungrateful, just like we could pick up another one at the grocery store.

The woman flashed us a big smile. "I'm Calista! I was gonna be MIT class of 2018 too, but I dropped out to have a kid." She winked at my wife, who just stared back like an idiot. *Jesus, please Ashley, get it together. This is our last chance.*

Mark, the older woman's husband, I guess, continued: "So we call ourselves headhunters, it's kind of a joke. When everyone else was raiding pharmacies, weapon stores, you know, our founder, Simon, collected the most important resource of all—human resources. Engineers, physicians, electricians, plumbers, building constructors, you know. Everyone with real skills. He found us in a radio tower. We had a greenhouse up there—Callie's always gardened—and I had a quite effective deterrent system set up. We kind of miss that place. We felt like the Swiss Family Robinson, but the city's much more comfortable. You wouldn't believe what we have. If the fresh fruit doesn't impress you, check this out!"

He took an iPhone out of his pocket and, shockingly, turned it on. Three out of four bars and the service was "Skynt". He was grinning, looking at my face. "Engineers tend to be sci-fi nerds."

After a pause, he continued: "So, this vehicle, tell me about it. These are solar panels from somebody's roof, right? But an F-350's not electric. I can't wait to see how you integrated the power system. We have some solar guys but they ran an installation business. They're excellent technicians, but we would love to work with a specialist engineer." He got up to walk around the truck. I knew I couldn't let him open the tool box. "So, where did you go to school?"

I cleared my throat. "I, uh, dropped out of community college." That was true. "I learned everything I know from YouTube videos." That was also true, but I didn't learn this electrical shit, I learned how to pit smoke. I was a line cook, Ashley a waitress. And in that tool box were the slow-smoked remains of the old man who had been driving this truck.

He reached his arm out to open it right away, of course. *Oh well, I guess we don't get to see his city, but Sarah can eat meat for another few weeks at least.* I took the axe out of my jacket, lifted my arm, and—felt it gripped by a strong hand. I turned around to face a big man, bigger than me. He was wearing body armor and had a rifle slung across his chest. Behind me, Mark spoke, "We always have more people than we introduce at first. Simon says, 'trust but verify.' You didn't build this truck, did you?"

"No, I didn't." *God, please...* "I can work though; I can do whatever you want. I don't have any pride. I'll dig ditches. If you need a cook, I can cook anything."

"We have more than enough laborers, and we don't take murderers." He was looking at the arm and half a leg. That was all that was left. "If you have cell phones, we'll buy them. We can pay you in produce, grain. We have jarred fruits as well. We would buy this truck, if you're willing to sell it, though that would be stupid of you. We won't steal it."

I turned to Ashley. She was looking at me with hatred and despair. She knew I had blown our chance. *I'm sorry I'm not a fucking smooth talker!* That woman was putting knitted socks on Sarah's blistered little feet.

Mark spoke again, "Also, it's part of our code—even if we won't take you, and we won't—we don't leave children to starve. If you want to send that little girl with us, she will be placed with a family. Everyone works, but it's easy work for kids. Weeding gardens, that sort of thing. And when she's old enough, there are plenty of intelligent young men, good providers, who would be happy to marry her."

"Not till she's grown up," the older woman repeated.

I looked at Ashley. Her face was wet. She took a breath and whispered, "Send her."

25

BLOOD AND EARTH

J.L. MACKEY

I've been climbing these smokestacks for going on twenty years. God, how the world has inverted since then.

I used to travel all over the Southeast; Texas to Florida to South Carolina, and sometimes even all the way up to Pennsylvania. Power plants, factories, paper mills. Making sure they were under their emissions limits. I thought we were pretty good stewards. Enviro didn't.

That's what they call themselves. Their logo is a globe with a drop of blood coming from it. Ain't that some shit? When I was a boy, environmentalists chained themselves to trees and called it a day. At least it seemed sincere. Now they'll derail your coal train and maybe put a sustainably-sourced bullet or two in your back. A bunch of them have been caught and jailed, but they either get off on technicalities with expensive lawyers, or get offed before trial.

They started out small. Then CO2 and methane levels shot up for a couple years. Some guy was pretty sure there had been a pocket of gas the size of Pittsburg under the sea floor that popped. He died in a car crash a week later. Then it was big farms, meatpacking plants, and any place with a smokestack. Didn't even matter if just water vapor was coming out of it. Oil refineries started looking like Kuwaiti oilfields afire. A war zone by any other name. Civil war with a biodegradable suit on.

Shit really got bad when power plants started going offline. The first ones to go were the coal-fired ones. Then the natural gas turbines. Railroads and pipelines are easy to bust, and control room operators aren't just born every day.

The government didn't do a whole lot. Nothing but speeches and prime-time pontificating. They did start paying people a million bucks a pop to put windmills up, but without the factories, those were hard to come by, too. A couple anti-domestic terrorism bills came up, but those were toothless, and politicians ended up doing what they always do: talk loudly, vote to give themselves pay raises, and then vacation together on whatever European island.

Nuclear plants are the only ones still standing. But when the fuel rods finally give out, who the hell knows. Even they have rolling blackouts with the high demands. You're lucky to get maybe four hours a day of power. Enough to keep the chest freezer going. And you'll pay through the nose for those four hours.

Didn't make much sense to keep testing emissions anymore when big rigs are getting ambushed on the highway and thousand-head herds are getting poisoned in the dark. Anyone with two brain cells to rub together knew what it was about. It was a royal fucking mess. Overnight, every privately owned firearm became a hired gun. Power company executives and big ranch owners had to travel like mob bosses, and being an Army or Marine Corps vet gets you hired for the task on the spot. The Afghanistan era snipers are treated like sports stars, traded back and forth to whoever is paying the most that month. They're getting old but they still got it, some of them still catching pink mist a half mile away. I heard a few of them have Hathcock-style bounties on their heads. State and local politicians didn't much like it, but what were they gonna do? No SWAT team in America has a combat vet on it, and National Guard stations are full of fat losers who are only there for the health benefits. Strange times.

So the local plant offered to triple my pay to stay up here, drop the testing equipment, and pick up some high-powered binoculars. Takes a certain kind of person to sit up this high all day and not lose it. You can see people from a long ways off, but they can see you, too. They gave me a rifle, too, but

I've never been much good with one, and surely not out to any real distance. The money is alright I guess, but it buys less every day. Not that I have a lot of time to spend it, and all.

Me and Dave do twelve-hour shifts. And it never ends. One climbs up, the other goes down. We exchange no words. Our faces have turned brown with sun, save for sharp circles around our eyes. Just us and the sun and the buzzards that sometimes land, looking for reprieve from their own damnation. Dave is a Marine Corps vet. He doesn't talk about it. I only know because of the tattoo on his left index finger. He touches a rifle like the rest of us touch a woman. I think he'd be fine to just live up here if they asked him to. Hell, he'd probably prefer it that way.

Hard to say where the world goes from here. Trying to think on it too much seems like a waste of time and another headache I don't need. I've heard some talk about people going scorched earth against Enviro. I don't know what that looks like, given that people are already getting killed. All I can think of is a Mexican cartel. Salting the fields, ending bloodlines. Medieval shit. Unsure if I'd like to live to see how it all ends. Maybe with a bang, maybe a whimper.

26

TREVOR

DOMINATED BY DIG DUG

COVID-42 was at its peak. For over the last twenty years, variations of the Wuhan-released Coronavirus had swept across the world every half decade or so. Some of the versions were a mere annoyance, some deadlier than the original COVID-19 strain. Society limped along. Many things people had earlier taken for granted had been replaced by rolling power outages, food shortages, lack of healthcare, and worse.

Trevor Engel wanted to help the world face the Coronavirus—but in his own way. First he went to school to become a nurse. After graduating, he worked in his hometown in clinics, ERs, and hospitals. His diverse skill set was in huge demand during the recurring pandemics. But it was time to move on.

Becoming a travelling nurse was the best thing Trevor ever did. Simply put, it lowered his chances of getting caught. Moving between jobs and states every eight weeks allowed him always new opportunities to practice his craft. He was never anywhere long enough for his co-workers or the pathologists or the coroners to suspect what he was up to. His temporary colleagues jokingly called him a "black cloud" or an "angel of death" because his patients always seemed to die unexpectedly. He laughed along. And why shouldn't they all die? He murdered them.

Trevor didn't see himself as a killer, but as an instrument in God's plan to ease suffering. Modern medicine, he believed, had an unhealthy and indeed unholy desire for length over quality of life. Doctors saw themselves as gods, and science gave them the tools to unnaturally prolong life. Open heart surgeries on ninety-five-year-olds, innumerable needless interventions, a never-ending stream of new medications. It was too much for Trevor. And aside from what he saw as his divine mission, there was the thrill of it.

Trevor's first was a ninety-three-year-old woman with advanced dementia. Paramedics had brought her to the ER from her memory care facility because the staff there thought she was acting strange. He took the report from EMS on their way in, noting how they said her baseline mental status was such that she didn't know her own name, had to be fed for all meals, wore diapers, and spent all day clutching a filthy baby doll. They added that she was medicated so that she wouldn't bite and scratch everyone. *That's not living*, thought Trevor.

They roomed her. Trevor went in and took a look at her—she didn't look good. He took her blood pressure: it was low and she was breathing rapidly. The female ER doctor, who sported they/them pronouns, asked him to start fluids and get labs. Trevor knew the doctor, fresh from residency, was likely going to intubate the patient. Trevor hung fluids and drew the labs, and with his needle still in her vein, he pulled from his pocket a large empty syringe, drew back on it, and injected a full load of air. He wasn't sure what would happen, but he had read that it could be fatal.

Unknown to him, she had a septal defect, and the air passed from the right to the left side of her heart, embolized to her brain, and immediately caused a massive stroke. Trevor saw her eyes roll back. She let out a moan and went into cardiac arrest. He called for help, assisted in the resuscitation effort, but it was to no avail. The ED doctor stopped resuscitation efforts after ninety minutes. Afterwards, Trevor felt numb. His soul was completely untroubled, he later realized. He then began to feel like an angel. He had helped that woman in her moment of greatest need.

Every few weeks Trevor bestowed such grace upon another soul. The more he helped shuffle off their mortal coil, the better he felt about himself. He was radiant. He felt a glow. And he got very good at killing people.

He quickly moved past air emboli to narcotic overdoses and potassium. Sometimes all it took was a simple pillow.

Next stop, Toledo—seventeen seniors. Another twenty-five in Indianapolis. Trevor wasn't sure of the exact count in Nashville. A few died right as he was injecting the special potassium mixture, so nature might have taken them before he could. But it was at least thirty. Next stop: Gary.

As far as Trevor could tell, he just got some ribbing from his colleagues. No one, not even once, ever asked him about what had happened to his patients. He expected some administrator somewhere to inquire, but none ever did! Trevor assumed that because his patients were already old and in critical condition, no one ever really cared to find out what actually killed them. Typically, he guessed, families did not ask for autopsies on their loved ones. Chalk up another death to COVID-42.

And so it went on for eighteen months, until the current iteration of the Coronavirus burned itself out. All told, world-wide deaths were in the hundreds of millions—this had been a particularly virulent strain. As fewer and fewer seniors were infected, travel nursing opportunities dried up, and Trevor felt less sure of his ability to get away with killing as many people as he had been doing for the last year and a half. He had honestly forgotten the total number by that point. It didn't matter.

Trevor returned to a full-time position in the ER he had started off in. He felt like a soldier returning home from the battlefront—scarred, but sure of himself. He knew that when COVID-46, or COVID-48, or any other Coronavirus returned, he would be ready for it.

Trevor Engel had become the Angel of Death.

27

DEMETER

DETECTIVE WOLFMAN

They had taken down all the crosses.

Special Agent Bennett Kemp had hated growing up down here in the Bible Belt and took his share of grim satisfaction when crosses and other Christian iconography were added to the list of prohibited hate symbols. But on this dark and lonesome stretch of highway, the ghostly white and unadorned church that loomed by his road block sent a small chill of dread through his veins. He turned back to the big rig that his team was swarming.

It was a 1975 Peterbilt 359 with a Mercury sleeper and a thirty-foot box. Agent Kemp ran his clammy hand over the red and black paint job to the custom name plate—DEMETER.

This rig had become a legend in the Bureau of Interstate Customs—his great white whale. It should have been decommissioned and put to scrap decades ago, but here it sat at the center of the most bizarre smuggling fiasco in all his years with the bureau.

Stolen shipments, missing trucks, drivers who seemed to disappear off the face of the earth. The only link was this rig. It had none of the standard GPS tracking systems or official registration and violated every energy policy in the book. Yet somehow this sore thumb had flown free under the radar for years.

Until now.

A scrawny deputy opened the sleeper and Kemp watched several pounds of dirt—Dixie red clay—spill out like an avalanche onto the officer. Kemp shined his flashlight inside and saw the sleeper was packed tight with the stuff. A whiff of the wormy earth traveled up his nostrils and down his spine.

Kemp found the driver at the back of the truck with Agent Dahl and several other deputies. The man was tall and lean with broad shoulders, muscular arms. He had a handsome, rawboned face. Kemp, like the rest of his team and most of the deputies, was squat and soft. Like an avocado with legs. He had seen old photos and movies of how people used to look. The driver may as well have stepped out of one of those old photographs. He even looked faded, somehow. His skin was tan yet pale all at once.

"You were supposed to stop at the weigh station on I-75 but you got off on the 411. Why did you do that?" Kemp motioned for one of the deputies to open the trailer. The driver adjusted the dirty ball cap that sat atop his long blond hair and grinned.

"Didn't want to be weighed," he said in a Carolina accent. He was staring at one of the deputies close by. A petite young woman. She was attractive, all things considered.

"Excuse me, darlin," the driver said. "You mind not pointing that gun at my head?"

"Don't call her *darlin*," Agent Dahl scolded. The stocky woman stepped up with her gun aimed at the driver's face. Kemp couldn't believe how poorly trained all these newer recruits were.

"No harm meant, ma'am," the driver said to Dahl. She looked as if he'd slapped her.

Kemp opened the trailer and climbed up. He and some deputies shined their lights over several large crates. Kemp lost his breath when they looked inside them.

A bust of Thomas Jefferson.

A statue of Robert E. Lee.

Paintings, writings, flags, even musical instruments. Contraband. Hate symbols. Each one of them had been cataloged and set for destruction but hijacked en route.

"Where are you taking these?" Kemp asked the driver. The man was still staring at the pretty deputy.

"Headed for Mobile," he said without taking his eyes off the woman. She seemed to be frozen, gazing back at him. "I got a contact in the port authority all set to ship them off."

"Ship them where?"

"South America, Eastern Europe. Anywhere they'll be safe."

Kemp couldn't help but chuckle. "You're very forthcoming," he said.

"No harm in it," the driver replied. "You ain't gonna tell nobody." He was still staring at the young woman and it was infuriating Agent Dahl.

"Stop staring at her," she commanded. Kemp ignored her. Something about what the driver said bothered him.

"What do you mean I won't tell anyone?"

"None of you are gonna leave here alive." The driver touched the deputy's cheek.

"I said stop looking at her!" Agent Dahl shrieked. Just then the driver turned to her and all of his good manners and charm were replaced by a glare of savage cruelty.

"Shut your cunt mouth, you fucking pig," he growled. And the pretty sheriff's deputy turned with a vacant expression and opened fire on Agent Dahl. A bullet ripped through Dahl's gaping mouth, taking several teeth with it, and exploded out the back of her skull. She let out a strangled sound like some kind of farm animal as she collapsed.

Kemp froze. The pretty deputy turned and shot him in the stomach. He fell out of the trailer and onto the pavement. It was still unbearably hot from the daytime sun. He could not turn over. All he could do was listen.

The screams. Desperate, gurgling, and abruptly silenced with a crunch or a tear. Finally the screaming stopped and Kemp heard footsteps approaching him.

"You know, I have to thank you, boss."

It was the truck driver. "I was *this* close to hanging it all up and catching a sunrise. Seen it all. Done it all. Then you folks came along and gave me purpose."

Kemp felt strong hands roll him over. The driver was soaked with blood from his mouth down to his belt buckle. His eyes had changed. They glowed like an animal's.

"What are you?" Kemp gasped.

"Me?" the driver said. "I'm history." He knelt by Kemp and flashed a grin full of fangs. "Now so are you."

Kemp cried out to God just before his windpipe was crushed and blood flooded his lungs. But God was not there.

They had taken down all the crosses.

28

THE ARENA MASTER'S SON

GLADIATOR

The Ten Paces dueling arena—licensed, bonded, and insured—upheld a great reputation despite the fact that it had the fewest registered deaths or injuries in the state. Conor McDivitt, the owner and operator, was always trusted to keep his word and do the right thing—even when those two choices conflicted.

But today, for the duel scheduled at 3:30, he considered throwing away his reputation and cheating the duel in favor of the challenged—his son.

Garreth, who turned eighteen only a month ago, was challenged by another high school senior over a girl.

Conor talked most duelists out of their challenges and into a settlement before the legal fight time and gave them a discount at his bar. When he couldn't, he presided over the event and made sure that all legal filings were complete and tight. These duelists dealt with death and injury, and they didn't need lawyers descending upon them while recovering.

The arena was 250 strides end to end, painted white except for the dark bullet-proof glass of the gallery and the orange doors for the duelists to enter. Seconds had their own booths and windows separate from the gallery which had an open com line to each other and to Conor's booth.

In the antechamber, Garreth racked the slide of his Glock. Conor stepped in and put a hand on his son's shoulder.

"Please, Garreth."

"Staying true to my word, like you taught."

"I taught you to turn down every fight you're challenged to. How many hours have we spent sparring so you could be ready for the cowards who can't settle things with words? I can pull the plug on this whole thing, say the arena has a safety hazard. I own this place and I will shut it down."

"Our seconds got us a backup."

"Why did you choose here?" Conor asked his son.

"He chose."

"He has no idea that your dad owns this place?"

Garreth stayed quiet, checking his pistol.

Conor crossed the arena to the challenger's antechamber.

The challenger, Jason, inspecting his pistol asked—"Is it time?"

"I do a final check with all of my duelists. One last opportunity to sign a settlement and get out. If they sign, I return their entire deposit, buy their first round at the bar, and give them half off their tabs. Do you know who I am?"

"The arena owner."

"Yes," Conor replied. "And do you know who is across from you?"

"My shithead opponent Garreth McDivitt."

"Do you know my name?"

"Conor," Jason responded.

"McDivitt," Conor finished.

"Oh."

"I want to give you some perspective. More perspective than I can give to most challengers. Your opponent, Garreth, my son, grew up here. He's seen more fights than you've dreamed of. His free time is spent with me at the training center I own next door. He can run, fight, and shoot better than half the instructors I employ. When you're thirty-six, and this fight is half your life behind you, are you going to remember why you did it? Would you die at age nine because someone at recess threw a fit? Would you kill a nine-year-old? Garreth can pump your guts full of lead before you hit the ground. That's not intimidation, it's fact. He's a demon with his Glock. So, Jason, will you please sign the settlement?"

Jason hesitated. "I'm the challenger. My honor—"

"Your honor's meaningless if you're dead. Live. Sign the settlement and live. Or don't, and face the arena master's son." Conor brought out the settlement papers.

A hesitant pause, then Jason took the papers. "Call in my second."

* * *

At the bar, after the papers were signed, a big, sloppy, pale, drunk barged through the gallery doors and shouldered Garreth out of the way.

"The hell is all this?" the big man demanded.

Jason's second piped up—"We've reached a settlement."

"Bullshit," the big man protested. He stomped toward Conor. "You trying to drag my son's name through the fucking shit? My family aren't a bunch of fucking pussies. You can't just talk them out of this without making him look a coward."

Conor stood silent.

"I will be damned if this arena drags my name through the shit," the big man huffed.

"Arena doesn't need to, your parenting has," Conor retorted.

"I challenge you, you asshole."

"For correcting a peer when he is making a mistake?"

"What mistake?"

"Allowing your child to think it's honorable to challenge another child to a duel to the death. If these boys wanted to fight to the blood, or three touches with a blade—fine. But you let your son walk around thinking that this was all worth dying for? I needed to correct you."

"Come on, coward. Duel."

"I don't duel."

The big man laughed. "The arena owner don't duel?"

"I've seen enough of them to know not to accept."

"You fucking worm! Fight me!"

Conor shrugged. "You aren't worth the trouble."

The big man steamed, and with his fist raised, rounded on Conor.

But his punch was slow. Conor ducked it. He spun into the big man and planted his hips across the big man's hips. Conor pulled on the over-extended arm and shoved his hips into the big man's midsection, throwing him into the air for a perfect toss. The big man went up and over, floated through the air, and came crashing into the cement floor face first, sending bits of teeth skittering across the floor. His arms and legs stuck out stiff and straight—the fencing response from traumatic force applied to the brain stem.

Now the police would be involved.

Conor knew it would be easier to duel these idiots and put them in their place instead of dealing with court dates and bureaucratic delays. Bureaucrats, however, didn't run the same risk of dealing injury and death, only assured boredom and incompetence.

But that was a price Conor was willing to pay.

29

RITE OF PASSAGE

BARBARIC DISCIPLE

There's nothing more unforgiving than the sun, the kid thought as he made his way down the crest of a mountain that overlooked a vast and barren desert. His cowboy hat was the only good decision he made for the journey. His white henley and tan pants were marred in sweat and dirt. The pack on his back made his traps burn as he carefully made his way to ground level. This was his rite of passage into manhood and he had a feeling he had found what the Fathers wanted him to see. Four days he had been on this path. Going west, always west, like the frontiersmen who came before him.

"Sometimes a man must do something that might kill him. To test himself, to find out if he's really alive," his father had told him. The words repeated in his mind as he passed through what could only be described as a valley of bones—but not just any bones. They were all severed right arms, arranged in a symbol around a heap of ruined war material. He knew what the symbol had been, what it had looked like, before the carrion and wild animals had gotten to it: the black sun. It was a sacrifice to God, made by his ancestors in the Holy War.

Though he was experiencing what must have been heat exhaustion, he felt the hidden power of this site. It heightened his awareness and all at once, he felt himself whisked back through time, the severed arms coming off the ground and re-finding their owners. But it was not through his eyes that he saw the terrible column making its solemn procession through the fierce and windy desert. It was through the eyes of his great-grandfather as he lay still underneath a shroud, camouflaged in the sand. He was waiting, waiting for the enemy force to draw near. For the right time to strike. For all the technological superiority of their enemy, his ancestor knew his opponents didn't have the will.

For all their rail weaponry, tanks, armored vehicles, drones, and even exo-skeletons, they didn't have the fight in them. Led into the desert against their will, against their better instincts. Now they walked into a trap. The kid could feel how his ancestor felt about them: an army of the deranged, relying too much on their "superior" technology. They believed technology would move man away from the battlefield, but it only gave the warrior another chance at what all men sought: undying fame.

An explosion crippled the lead tank, another the tank at the end of the column as rail rounds hit the enemy hard. They took some casualties, but they were made for this kind of warfare. The distances had to be closed. It was time for his ancestor to prove his worth. He and his squad broke their cover, sprinting towards the enemy column.

In olden times, it was insanity to run into machine gun fire, but this was what his ancestors did. As the fire turned toward them, the kid's forefather activated a device in his left hand that emitted an energy shield around him like a sphere, negating the enemy's fire entirely. His team rallied behind him, picking off easy targets as they broke through no man's land.

Once they made it past the enemy's armor, the slaughter began. He cut the distance to the nearest soldier, who tried to flee to reload. The kid's ancestor let the shield down and shot his short-barreled railgun into the man's chest. The shield turned back on as he covered the flank of his team, while they pacified the men in the next armored truck.

The kid saw what happened next: A soldier in an exo-skeleton caught their flank, killing two of his great-grandfather's friends; the brutal battle that ensued with the man whose exo-skeleton gave him the strength of Heracles. Even without the suit, he was a beast of a man. But his forefather fought with the excellence of Achilles and despite being beat down badly, he got his man with a Bowie knife through the skull. The battle winded down as his ancestor, covered in blood, took in the chaos around him. What was past became the present again. The kid, breathing heavily, realized the divinity wasn't done with him. Blood surged through his veins. He glimpsed what was coming.

The kid—now a man—sat on a spaceship in the stratosphere with a railgun. There were many such ships in a holding pattern as detonations and mushroom clouds appeared over a continent before them. Then, he was taken further into the future. He and his men watched the first of many ships embark into space, into the final frontier. They would be following them soon after. Mankind finally doing what it was meant to do. The Imperium into the great unknown.

Just as quickly as the vision took him, the kid was back to reality, staring at the heaping rubble of war material as the sun set on the horizon. He had been given purpose—from the wild God Himself. The vision imparted a lesson he was never to forget: No matter how far greatness took his people, it was important to not give in to the hubris that came after it, to not get comfortable, never lose their edge. Always, his eyes had to be set onwards.

30

GENESIS REVELATION

MENCIUS MOLDBUGMAN

Blood, the blood of weak men, the blood of men cowering wild-eyed with final shameful breath, dripped from the ancient wooden walls of the longhouse. Death covered every space. Here, in the midst of death, stood life, ascendant in the warrior. He had cast the weakness from the dark prison with his glistening sword. The women, doe-eyed but dangerous creatures that had inflicted this fate upon their men through decades of suffocation, shivered with awareness that their machinations could no longer keep aloft the walls of their false Elysium.

With purpose, the warrior strode towards the nearest woman and grabbed her. Her men dead and with no aid at hand, the woman leaned back and opened her legs, offering herself to her new master. Her sex thanked him for his strength and moistened with relief that her reign had finally come to an end. The other women took heed and did the same: the longhouse that had once strangled the seed of male energy now opened itself to it.

The warrior lay with the woman, then with the others. They wept tears of joy when his firm hand gripped their necks—all except one old crone too bitter and barren to bear the blessings of his fruit, and who in her jealousy resented the warrior for revealing the truth of her ugliness. As the last of her sisters moaned under the presence of the warrior, she prayed to Gaia and cast her staff amidst the flesh of the fallen menfolk. The crone opened up the entrails and revealed their secrets to the watching warrior.

"Son of Apollo," she cried, "gaze upon your past and future and repent! No utopia awaits you after the war!"

And the warrior looked and saw the beginning of all things. Yet here were no Gods or Titans or even Ouranos claiming the Earth. Here instead was Father Chaos who held the elements in one infinitesimally tiny point of roiling energy. Life emerged not from a yawn, but a bang—a Big Bang louder and greater than all the battle cries that had ever been and ever would be. That Bang, that Divine Spark, expanded instantly into the void, creating matter where before nothing had existed. Onwards it roared for near-eternity; a great unstoppable tide of energy exploding into life *ex nihilo*. Galaxies flared and formed as the Great Vitality continued growing, living, creating. Worlds cooled and gave birth to life. Monstrous volcanoes spewed lava, in turn bringing lightning and fire. It was neither Zeus nor Prometheus that brought these gifts to the world, but the remorseless hammer of energy crashing down on every corner of the long universe where before had only been gloom.

On some planets animals appeared. On some planets one animal stood tall amongst the others and this animal was Man. Here the warrior saw his own story woven within the grander tapestry of All Things. Man rose out of the primordial dawn, stepped out of his shadowy cavern, and built cities and art and war and music and poetry and all the beautiful things that men could build. He saw himself in that moment—the only moment that mattered—ensuring the glory of his people for centuries to come. His children stepped out into the world as energy had once streamed out into the emptiness countless millennia before, until all the Earth radiated with the fruits of their grandeur; their shining cities reaching out for the very stars themselves.

"Watch closer," whispered the crone. "See what happens to the dream of Man."

The entrails moved. The world turned. A blind maggot reared its head from the intestines and gnawed upon the rotting meat. The universe reached its peak; energy diminished then disappeared. The bright lights of supernovae faded until only the grim scythe of entropy remained. Man had reached a similar fate long before: his cities overwhelmed with greed and weakness, his people fleshy and lazy, his shiny toys first weakening then replacing. The spirit weakened, struggled under its own weight. Minds grew as fat as the shells carrying them and the great cities began to fade like extinguished stars. The whole world was once again plunged into darkness and from the ashes all that remained, waiting, was the longhouse. The eternal longhouse. The universe retreated in upon itself, black holes consumed matter, existence became tighter and smaller, but the longhouse would take in the shivering refugees. The longhouse would take all within its walls, though cared nothing for what possibilities lay outside.

The crone laughed triumphantly.

The warrior laughed too.

For the warrior looked deeper than the crone.

Though the maggot feasted on the entrails of the dead enemy, the warrior could see that from the rotten remains new life would pour back into the Earth. From the Earth would grow new harvests to feed new warriors who would pick up their ancestors' sword and continue their work. The universe contracted, the world of men contracted, the galaxies withered, matter dispersed, cities fell, and men disappeared. All was lost... entropy, endless entropy... darkness closed in... until...

"NO!" screamed the crone.

"YES," spoke the warrior.

The shrinking universe collapsed within itself, then in a divine instant of shattering explosive power, was reborn. It rushed outwards faster than ever before, reclaiming every inch of its lost territory. Stars flowered. Worlds bloomed. Man once more stepped out of his cave to take what was rightfully his.

The warrior stepped out of the longhouse, loyal mothers to his future sons in tow. With one graceful movement, he threw his torch towards the stinking remnants of the wooden cage and watched patiently until only the dim embers remained and the screams of the old woman could no longer be heard.

31

THE ORDER OF ALL THINGS RESTORED

CRUSADER

The sound of the buzzing bees fills my sunburnt ears. The dew of morning's grass clings to its host. The sun shines through the fog as I approach the hives.

The calming noises of nature keep the flood from sweeping over me. The tall grass shields my view below my belt. I step onto a snake. It hisses and bites my exposed calf.

I see that it is a rattlesnake. Not good.

I try to squeeze the venom out with my fingers, only making things worse. I yell for help; my squad carries me to a tree. After all the battles I fought, it might be nature itself that claims me. My vision blurs. Two soldiers prop me up and we head for a medical tent about five miles south.

It begins to rain with heavy winds. The rain fills my already water-logged boots. Mud cakes to the bottom, making every step an annoyance. We approach a field just off the road where a small stream winds down to an old abandoned stone quarry. The birds are still singing the songs of creation despite the shuddering cold. I look up to the sky and the rain acts as a purgation of my sins of yesterday.

I try to clear my eyes to look at the rusted winding metalwork of the once-working quarry. The old world fades under the corrosive march of time. All monstrosities melted down: the last of their flags only recognize fire and ash. The remnants of those foolish enough to wage a Holy war against us have all been cast aside. The mother's womb now filled with everything right and just.

We no longer dwell in the darkness, the spirit no longer faint. Despair has turned into a righteous walk of truth. This quarry will work again making buildings and statues that accentuate the masculine form, paralleling the foundation of humanity, erecting man-made monoliths reaching Heaven's gates. Man reaching to his creator with outstretched, calloused hands saying *thank you*.

We did not return to the old world. We couldn't. The fire within created something new.

A sense of warmth washes over me, either death or rebirth. There is still much more work ahead. I smile as a gust of wind pushes my body towards the medical tent. They tell me I will recover in about a week's time. I have never felt more alive. Our enemies erased; we have restored the order of all things. The one who pays heed to the wind will never sow, and the one who watches the clouds will never reap. He has reached his hand from on high and delivered us from the deep mire. He has rescued us from the hands of wicked foes. We have won.

32

TWO DREAMS: A CRYPTIC DIPTYCH

GABRIEL MAMOLA

I. Platonic Dialogue

I received a call from an old lover. She had been having dreams, she said, having to do with the name Lilith, and did I know anything about it, anything more concrete than the common musical associations. Her tarot had been unforthcoming, and she had a rule against consulting the bots in spiritual matters...

GABRIEL
I do know who Lilith is. She was the first wife of Adam from Genesis, but she isn't in Genesis. She is a legend, a myth from the Kabbalah.

NATALIE
Adam's first wife? But not Eve?

GABRIEL
Before Eve. The legend says that the first wife God made for Adam was not a woman, but a spirit, an angel or daemon in a female form. God named her Lilith and gave her to Adam, but she resented flesh and resented serving a

man of flesh in marriage. So she rebelled and Adam drove her off. That's when God made Eve.

NATALI
I've never heard that before. So why am I dreaming about her?

GADRIEL
I don't know. But she's a very ancient feminine archetype, I think. She's probably hiding in every woman's unconscious somewhere. Maybe every girl thinks of herself as Lilith sometimes.

NATALIL
Do you think of me as Lilith?

GADARIEL
It was your dream, not mine! But no, I don't see you that way. There were other good reasons for us to break up. It was for the best.

NATALILI
What do you mean, exactly?

GADAMRIEL
Exactly? I don't think I could say exactly. But why did you call? Was it to talk about your dream or to swim in the water under the bridge?

NATALILIT
I don't know. But I think you definitely saw me as Lilith in some way.

GADAMREL
Maybe while we were breaking up. There were certainly times, in the real thick of it, when I felt I was talking to something through you, something bigger and older than you.

NATALILITH
I believe in the old gods.

GADAMEL
I know.

NATLILITH
I think people can be visited by the gods, or afflicted, if it's a negative thing.

GADAME
Perhaps in some sense.

NALILITH
Was Lilith a god? Or a goddess, I mean?

GADAM
Some people interpret her as a revamped Egyptian goddess, maybe Isis, that the Hebrews recast negatively as a succubus when Moses and the Patriarchs moved in. Some see her as a logical counterpart to the devil, the feminine side of evil, the female non serviam. Others take her for a kind of proto-feminist archetype.

ALILITH
Who do you think I am?

ADAM
Off...

LILITH
!

II. The Dream of Scipio

I forgot to mention it, but I too had dreamed a dream, wherein I, unstuck in time, saw into dagum yet to come, when ROME the Great, Eternal City, Seat of Empire was rebuilded out of the nano-ash. Some called it Galabraxas, others Golganooza or Babylon Again, but there is only one true City of Man and it is everlastingly Rome.

This City was Man's truest mistress & most lasting lover, for she signified PAX. She was Commodity & Concord & Common Good. She was Civilization & Science & Exercise of Virtue.

Not Rome the First, not the Christian nations in their multiplicity, not even we ancients who called down the fire from Heaven, had known such justice in stability. All men who had survived the Great Philtre (or who had survived as Men) were declared Citizens of the Empire & Children of God, their wives & clans & children along with them.

I saw the Romans extend their dominion over Eordan's civilizational waste, until it covered all the Vir-Eld, from the temperate South Pole to the North Polar Okean, so that they called the planet "Eordan Nostrum," Our Earth, & the walls of this Rome were the atmosphere itself, but she looked to spread her inevitable Empire over even the Seven Seeds planted in the Field of Arbol.

As for us the living, their ancestors, they understood only scraps & fragments, for we had made ourselves wonderfully and terribly strange by the End. With regard to our mastery over Nature, some Cyberpunk St. Thomas of their own age might have written in his commentary on the *Exegesis of St. Phillip of Antioch, CA.*

"De Informatione: The transmittance of information through material is the aim of the Alchemical Art, which is the greatest Art for this reason, that man by nature desires to know, & the art of Alchemy [hacks] the wisdom of the ancients, of whom is said they possessed technique to a preeminence, & who by art recorded their technique within the changeable but everrepeating patterns of elemental matter, which art is said to be what is meant by the cypher COMPUTOR."

They knew something of the poets, of ELIOT's greatest drama, *History of Aragorn, King of Gondor*, something of STONE-COLD F. AUSTIN's *Pomp & Psychopomp*, & of the *Two-thousand and One Space Odysseys* of HOMER (which includes such well-known tales as "The Assassination of Captain Kirke By The Coward Ishmael"), & *The Heavenly Hierarchies of Those Grievous Angels* of PSEUDO-GRAM PARSONS.

I, dreamreader, watched as the Romans rediscovered aerodynamics & combustion & more, & used this knowledge to construct rockets red as the blood of Uncle Remus & within these rockets ventured beyond the atmospheric borders of Eordan Nostrum.

The first world to surrender to the legions of Roman rockets & their Space Marines was hollow Byzantium, satellite of Eordan, and certain it is that the Men of Byzantium were like the Men of Rome & remembered the ancients & their sacred rites & the Vir-Eld before the Philtre. The Men of Byzantium knew also of the DATUM we ancients had embedded bit-fully in the very quanta of matter, & of the crafting of the COMPUTOR & other philosopher's systems according to the Rule of Elbertus Magnusk.

& I dreamed that after the Renaissance bestowed upon them by the hacking of our ancient Alchemystery, the Romans sailed on solar winds to Barsoom where, according to all the ancient texts, they expected to find a people dark & golden eyed who lived in houses of crystal pillars & wore bronze masks into battle on six-legged steeds before the gates of ancient atmospheric factories on the edges of a dead Okean. But instead they found only dust & wind, as though the journey from planet to planet had been but a passage from dust to dust.

To find a dead planet, moreover one that had never cradled life at all, was a grave scandal to the faith of the Romans, who believed in a historical Mars no less than historical Eden, Babel, Albion, Gondor, and Jerusalem. After all, it was an old & venerable tradition that held Mars to be the place of a righteous but imperfect SOUL's purgation, that Mt. Purgatory was the true name of Olympus Mons, & that the Oyarsa of Mars was an archangel of the first rank. But to find the place of the SOUL's work empty? To find that the ancient histories of Mars, the works of the Spiritual Masters, to find even these were a parable at best & a lie at worst? The cracks in the edifice of Roman Scholasticism, & in the study of the ancient writings, soon widened into what became the Martianist Heresy.

& each believing Roman who travelled to Mars to see the wasteland for himself found it was grief, & not disillusionment, that he suffered when he saw nothing but yellowgray & blackred dustclouds covering the planet of his dreams, & þæt wæs rōd awakyning.

33

THE FIVE HUNDRED

LYCURGUS

It began when a moment of divine clarity found a few daring souls. All the noise of the current day fell silent, and they could finally imagine themselves standing before the gate to Grand Politics. Two massive, thirty-foot stone doors stood bolted shut, but when they approached and pressed the side of their faces against the stone, they could catch the slightest razor-edge glimpse of what was on the other side.

A thousand and one sensitive young men had come before to this exact point, yet the new adventures and noble destiny on the other side remained sealed off. Now, the men were different and uniquely constituted: they were made with more of that material which formed the older GREEK IDEAL. No more theorizing, no more chasing petty outrages; no more setting insignificant goals: politics was understood to be a contest for *mastery*. For them, everything was rendered down to a very simple question: "Who rules?" And the answer to that question became equally clear: "Not us."

At once, these men took stock of the realities in front of them, affirmed a handful of humble truths, and hatched their plot.

They knew that even their hero Odysseus had been a slave to circumstances and could not exact his revenge until the moment was just right. The truest and best solutions require patience and careful preparation. It can be a fatal mistake to become desperate for action. Cunning and organizing genius are rare qualities that must not be squandered—they must stalk the opportune moment and accumulate in power until they can spring forth and score a great victory. Fortunately for these few daring souls, circumstances were favorable, and their country was ripe to receive the next monumental chapter in its history.

In 2026, Donald Trump's second term was in full swing. While he achieved some success on critical issues like border security and trade, his administration was stalling out just as it had done the first time around. Every significant executive policy aimed at deconstructing the deep state and holding America's domestic enemies accountable was held up by leftist judges. The media continued to oppose him at every turn, and his own party was once again doing him no favors. The usual jackals could not resist making a buck off saying, "See! Told you so! Should have gone with DeSantis back when we had the chance!" (DeSantis' credibility with the MAGA base was destroyed after his failed primary attempt in 2024, and his popularity tanked after the story came out connecting DeSantis with the same unpleasant circles in D.C. that Rubio was also tied up in.) It became clear that the limits of presidential populism under Trump had been reached and its goals were in danger of being left unfulfilled. America's "MAGA moment" was sunsetting and the grey status quo was poised to poison *life* for hundreds of years ahead.

The plan going forward was incredibly simple: identify and assemble the best men. So, the initial few began to survey their country and sought out 500 men most worthy of the honor to rule. Each of these men were successful, possessed practical skills, and were capable of commanding. Most importantly, they were all healthy and handsome! Individually, they carried a kind of magnetism and natural gravitas that served them well under the old regime, but their potential had always been confined to the *banausic* realms of business and bureaucracy. No amount of career accolades or wealth could compensate for the fact that they were not really their own men. Politics and power were always denied to them by inferior types, and they now felt wronged by this. It was only by bringing them into the fold together that they came to possess a kind of power that needed no proving. Simply lining themselves up against the current "elites" and rulers in both political parties made their superiority self-evident in every regard.

Things really took off when the Five Hundred began meeting together in congresses all over the country. They rented extravagant and historic venues to discuss privately matters of the most import to the future of the nation. Everywhere they went, intrigue and attention followed. They marketed themselves brilliantly and played to all the media's weaknesses.

"Who are these people?"

"What are they up to?"

"Can you believe who we saw there!"

They selectively released information, and an entire network of aligned organizations and individuals naturally formed to help propagandize their cause. Over time, many started looking to the Five Hundred for leadership. It can be hard to remember how desperate people were back then, but nobody alive had ever experienced real political leadership. So when the Five Hundred seemingly appeared out of nowhere overnight, it felt as if a race of lost Atlanteans had emerged from the deep. Within a few months, their right to rule became undeniable.

The genius of the Five Hundred was that they had effectively positioned themselves as a legitimate alternative waiting on the sidelines. The old regime did not have the will or popular support to do anything about this, and ultimately everything the Five Hundred was doing was completely legal. Being ready to take over the Republican party, to create a new party to replace the GOP, or just being prepared to serve the will of the people at a moment's notice is not a crime.

Today we can reflect back and debate the approach the Five Hundred eventually decided on, but the more important thing to remember is how this whole idea turned out to be much easier than anyone would have ever thought. Extensive care and foresight were given up front during the selection, but once the Five Hundred were assembled, everything just kind of took care of itself. They whipped the scoundrels and reconstituted the American people. These men asserted their right to rule and had no bad conscience about it. They took possession of themselves and threw open the doors to Grand Politics.

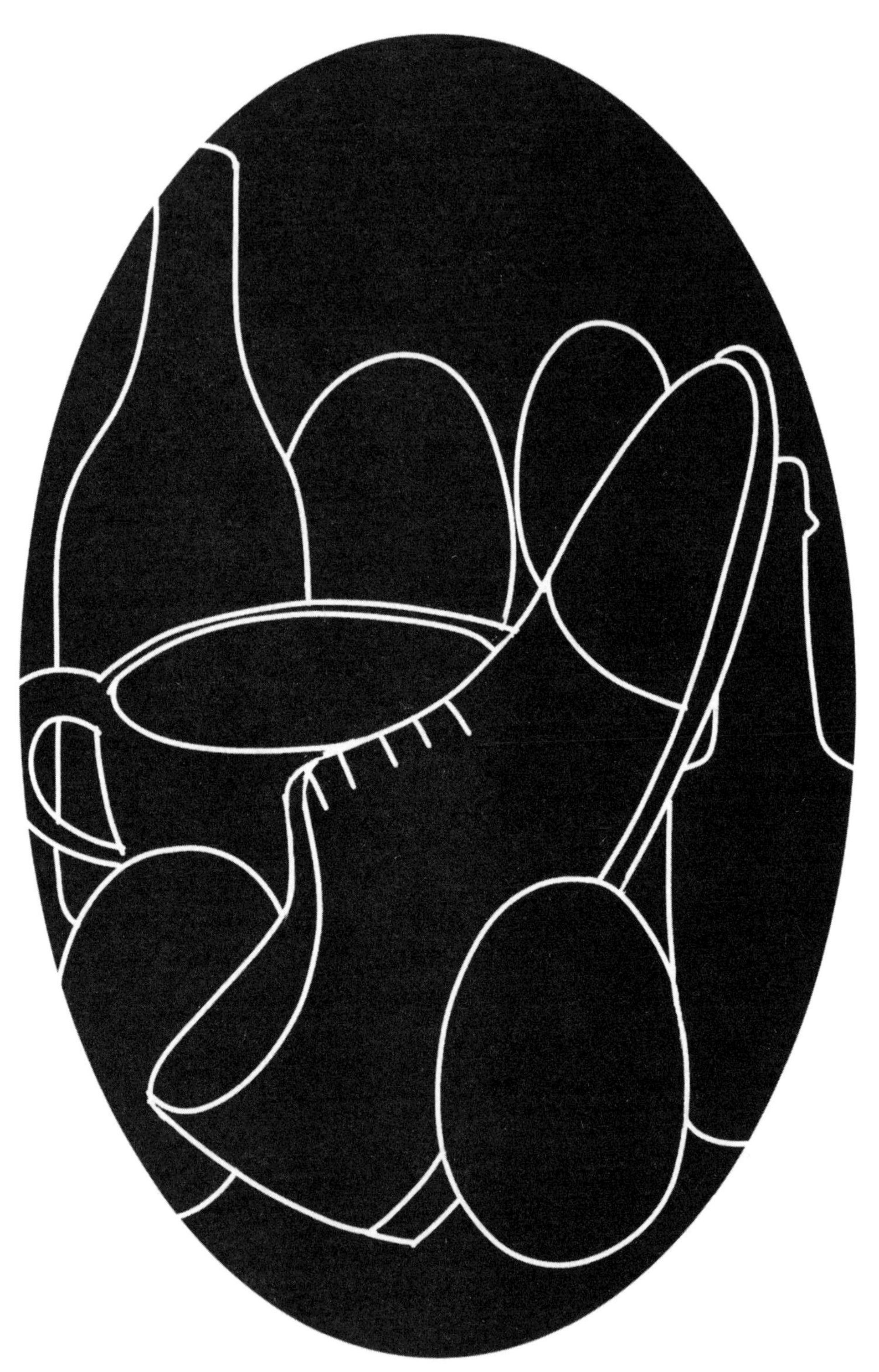

34

PIZZA BOY

RAW EGG NATIONALIST

Once upon a time, around about when things finally started to go right, this New York office space, all 20,000 square feet of it, had been the headquarters of a magazine called *Rolling Stone*. Nobody talked about *Rolling Stone* any more these days—in fact, they'd stopped talking about it long before it folded—but for a while it was considered the future of popular magazine journalism. A heady, exciting mix of music, politics and culture, unlike anything that had come before. That was the late 1960s. A very different time in America.

A very different time for the world.

Now that the stone had well and truly stopped rolling, the moss could finally begin to gather. There was a new magazine in town, full of promise. Its name was MAN'S WORLD.

The CEO of that promising magazine, a British gentleman who used to go by the anonym "Raw Egg Nationalist" (and sometimes still did, largely for reasons of nostalgia), was in his office. John Winthrop—for that was his name—wore an exquisite chalk pinstripe suit from Huntsman of London, John Lobb shoes from Jermyn Street, a shirt from Budd's of Piccadilly and a yellow silk tie he'd picked up from Boggi in Milan. No pocket handkerchief—of course.

His silver lapel pin bore the slogan, "Barron for Chancellor 2032".

He turned from the full-length window and pressed a button on the desk. After a harsh buzz, he was greeted by the far more pleasing sound of his secretary's voice.

"Yes, Mr Winthrop? How can I be of help?"

"Eva, I'd like a double espresso, an ice-cold bottle of San Pellegrino"—*Sol Brah's orders*—"and six duck eggs in a pint glass with a shot of tabasco."

"*Of course*, Mr Winthrop."

He loved the emphasis. Eva was charming, beautiful. Dutch. She was the best hire he'd ever made.

He ordered the same thing every day, three times, and three times every day she'd enter the room a few minutes later bearing a little tray with his drinks on it. The drinks were always, without fail, perfect—the espresso topped with a rich silky crema, the sparkling water as cold as if it had been retrieved direct from an alpine stream, the quantity of tabasco just enough to cut through the richness of the pastured duck eggs—but really it was the way she delivered them. The almost unbearable sexual spark she was able to ignite in her progress from door to desk. The way she laid out the drinks in front of him on three BPA-free paper coasters, her breasts drawing near to his face as she leaned across him. The little smile she gave before turning. And then the long walk back to the door, affording him plenty of time to study her tight little ass from Nijmegen or wherever it was the Dutch were growing all of these incredible blondes.

Not a word was ever said during this thrice-daily ritual.

The man formerly known as Raw Egg Nationalist chewed on the thought of Eva in her short pencil skirt for a few minutes, while he waited for her customary *rap-rap-rap*.

You can imagine his surprise, then, when instead of Eva's gentle ingress the door was practically kicked off its hinges. A man appeared in the doorway, sweating and attired in a manner that could only be described as "comically dishevelled". The interloper swept across the floor to the desk with the grim resolve of one of those terminally harassed waiters that work St Mark's Square in the summer months. It was warm in the building; but no man had any right to be perspiring to this extent.

"Your, uh, drinksh, uh, Mishter, uh, Winshrop," he spluttered, with an accent that placed him somewhere south or perhaps east of the Alps. Rome or Romania—it wasn't clear. The man presented the tray on one hand, tucking his other hand behind his back and bowing forward with a perfunctory bit of mock-ceremony. An unnerving approximation of a smile spread across his face.

Something about this chap seemed familiar...

"Yes. Well... er, thank you for that." Winthrop removed the drinks, one by one, from the tray, doing his best to keep his distance, and placed them directly onto the antique green leather of what had once been his grandfather's writing desk.

As he peered into the espresso cup and tried to fathom its contents, he noticed that the fellow hadn't moved an inch. There he was, standing in the same spot with the same forced look of... whatever it was plastered across his face.

"Is there something else?"

"The dishident right!" he exclaimed, standing up straight and raising a finger as if in revelation.

"Come again!?"

"The dishident right!" the man exclaimed a second time, finger still raised.

"The dissident right!?" That was a phrase Winthrop hadn't heard or used for some time.

"Yesh. I wash in the dishident right, jusht like you. I ushed to hath a magathine, jusht like you."

Winthrop squinted at him for a moment. Aha! He remembered! Back in the early days that savagely balding pate had been the beginnings of a Norwood 5, and the grossly distended belly a mere paunch, but still it was unmistakably—*him*. Now, *what was his name?*

"Well, well," Winthrop said uneasily. "How far the mighty have fallen! Time is a cruel mistress and all that. I jest, of course. How are things... er... *my friend?*"

"Itsh been up and down. But I'm shtill writing and publishing. Shtill looking to make it big. Here..." The man began fishing around frantically in his trouser pockets, which only added to the impression of a demented vagrant. Winthrop made a note to himself to have a panic alarm installed under the desk.

At last, with immense satisfaction, the man presented a pile of crumpled papers and set them down next to the drinks.

The CEO of MAN'S WORLD leaned forward. It was a cheaply printed pamphlet with a meaningless title that was impossible to pronounce. "Art and Literature for the New Dissident Mainstream" ran the subtitle. Winthrop bit his lip and began turning the pages.

He counted the words "Operation Paperclip" at least four times. "Dreaming of Trumpwave". "The New Blackpilled Bad Boys". Something about Dua Lipa. This was the same drivel this chap had been publishing ten years ago, to no discernible effect.

"You'll read it?"

Winthrop looked up at the man, and was greeted, to his surprise, by the face of a child. At this moment he knew the wrong word could, quite literally, be fatal.

"Yes, I'll read it. I'll let you know what I think. Give my secretary your details and I'll be in contact. Now, I have work to be getting on with—once I've enjoyed this *delicious* coffee, of course."

The man smiled and then stood to attention, performing a little salute. As he reached the door, he looked back and said, "I knew you would like isht!"

Winthrop studied the contents of the espresso cup again, then put his hand on the glass bottle of sparkling water. *Warm*. He didn't even look at the eggs.

Satisfied that the man would now be on his way out of the building, he pressed the buzzer for the second time that day.

"Yes, Mr Winthrop? How can I be of help?"

"Eva, I don't ever want to see that man again."

There was a short pause.

"Yes, Mr Winthrop. You never will. Is there anything else?"

"No, Eva. That's all. Actually—wait. I'd like a double espresso, an ice-cold bottle of San Pellegrino, and six duck eggs in a pint glass with a shot of tabasco."

35

SCHOOL OF SOL

ABDULLAH YOUSEF

The oak wood door bashed open. Two school guards rushed into the empty dorm room. A warm draft entered the open wood-framed window, ruffling the 100 percent linen curtains.

"He's gone already."

"Search the room, he's got to have left something behind."

Both guards were fair-skinned, veiny men with beach tans. Carotene-maxxed. Each was dressed in loose polo shirts and hand-sewn caps that read the same: SOL SECURITY. They proceeded to tear the dorm room apart for evidence, looking for anything to get a lead on where the suspect and his accomplice ran off to. The first guard tore apart a silk pillowcase and threw the lavender-scented bed sheets across the room. The second guard opened the mini fridge. Raw milk. Berries. A few slices of 100 percent grass-fed organic steaks from cows that were kept in red-light vaults five hours a day.

"Well, at least he's not a PUFA Poofster."

"That'd be the least of his crimes. Come on, there's nothing here."

They exited the dorm room and jogged across the hall, where the glass roof showed the country's largest palm trees leaning ever so slightly over the building. Two students were busy re-lathering a bronze statue of Apollo in coconut oil.

"Hail Sol, brothers," one of the students said, throwing a Roman salute.

"Hail Sol!" the guards shouted back, throwing a Roman salute as they ran past.

All around the hallways, staircases, and classrooms there were open windows where different berry plants and herbs grew into the building. The first guard sneezed after he almost got hit by an untrimmed oregano bush. After sneezing, he took out one of the syringes in his belt and injected himself with it: vitamin E oil. They passed dozens of students on their way, and each hailed them just the same. Why wouldn't they? Not doing so was an instant penalty of forty pushups, thirty burpees, and a forced feeding of a tablespoon of canola oil.

They made it to the main atrium. There was a twenty-foot-tall statue of one of their patrons, saint and savior Raymond Peat. He was decked in hoplite armor and swastika jewelry, wielding a giant carrot pointed at the sky. His shield had an emblem of a cup of coffee.

For some reason, the oil lanterns were all shut off when they went in. The sun hadn't set just yet, and in the distance they saw someone they recognized. They bolted for him.

The kid seemed not to have skipped his sprint training since he ran fast, but the second guard was able to catch up and tackle him to the ground in the staircase.

"Where's your friend? You helped him escape, didn't you?"

"What, who?"

"Brett. The vile boy has disgraced himself and must be adjudicated immediately before the Sol Council."

"I don't know what you're talking about! What did he even do?" the kid yelled, trying to resist further.

The guard, now on top of him, took a scanner from his belt and put it to the kid's forehead. Cortisol level of 15 mcg/dL.

"Unacceptable. Do you realize what being implicated in his crime means?"

The first guard crouched next to him. "That's right, you don't know?"

"I don't. Please, he didn't do anything wrong, I'm sure of it. Brett is one of the best of us, man! I once saw him slonk an ostrich egg whole. You know how big those things are?"

"Where is he? You're coming up on at least fifty cycles in the artificial light chamber."

"No, please!"

"That's right. Maybe we'll coat you in a polyester blanket while you're in there."

"OH GOD, PLEASE! Okay look, I think I saw him running down Thule Boulevard with his girlfriend just now, but that's it!"

The guards looked at each other, then back at the sweating student. "Alright then."

They let him go and stood up. The student looked around. "What the hell are you even chasing him for?"

The guards were already marching away. One of them looked back with horrific disgust. "We've been informed he was intimate with his lady friend at the sister school, and that he'd... he'd..."

The other guard spoke up. "He blew his essence instead of retaining it."

The friend of the accused was struck with a cold expression. Within a matter of seconds, he accepted Brett's fate and nodded to the guards.

One of the guards took out a device shaped like a pen. He raised it to the student's eye level and pressed a button. Suddenly the entire staircase was blasted with a flash of red light. They continued onwards as the student stared at the wall, confused, wondering where he was and how he got there.

They ran outside to their cruiser. Tacky old thing, but it did the job. They sped out of the parking lot and drove down Apollon Lane, past the thirty-foot-tall statue of Sol Brah.

It was made of stone, carved with autistic precision by the nerd slaves made captive after the great war. It modeled his physique after how his fans remembered him—chiseled chest and abs, toned arms and capped shoulders, fully capturing the lanky nature of his overall build. They meticulously carved out his long hair, framing a face which... no one really knew. They settled for a literal interpretation. A pixelated face carved out of stone, like something built in fucking Minecraft.

The second guard loaded up his shotgun as they got closer to Thule Boulevard. Non-lethal ammunition.

Soon Brett would learn the consequences of his disgraceful actions.

36

PERSON OF LORDLY CALIBER

MUSTACHE BALDIE

The castle imposed itself on the evening landscape. From the air, Isabel saw the lush canopy of the forest drop abruptly away to open up for the grounds surrounding the structure, illuminated by hidden lights under bushes, behind walls and gardens and outbuildings and the barracks. The shadows of men patrolling in pairs or alone stretched out along the grass.

The pilot cut to the side, swooping down and around towards the landing pad. She wondered if Lord Smith had instructed the pilot to do this for her benefit. Shot of adrenaline before dinner. Or maybe the pilot wanted to show off a bit for her. He'd certainly flirted the whole first half of the flight. They landed softly, and she disembarked with the pilot's help. Two armed guards escorted her on either side up the paved path towards the residence.

At the door, a guard she'd never met before stopped her and stood in a human T, arms to each side, indicating he needed to search her.

"Really?" She thrust her hip to the side, exposing her thigh just so through the cut of her yellow evening dress. The dress clung to her body perfectly, skin tight. Nothing to hide.

"Really," he said. He pulled out a magnetic wand and waited for her to humiliate herself. She humphed, and assumed the position of a searchee, something she hadn't done since before the revolution. At the airport they used to line everyone up like cattle. Even kids.

He waived the wand, and it sang a tinny pitch as it passed over her wrists and elbows, down her sides, and then up the inside of her thighs. She grabbed it right before he pressed it to her crotch.

"Excuse me," she said and thrust it away. He smirked and stepped aside to let her in.

Lord Smith came into the dining hall alone. She curtsied for him, and he kissed her on her neck.

"You smell lovely," he said. "Are you hungry?"

"Starving! It was a long flight. Who is that new guard?"

"Just a precaution."

Two servants helped them seat and two more appeared with the first course.

"Well, he was *extremely* rude," she said.

Lord Smith put his fork down. "How so?"

Isabel shuddered. She felt power over the fate of the poor recruit. It thrilled and frightened her. Every hair on her body stood up, and she contemplated the fact that whatever she chose, leniency or punishment, would be an exercise in total control of his fate.

"Oh, nothing. It's just I couldn't believe he insisted on searching me, is all," she said and waved her hand. "I guess I was exaggerating. He wasn't so bad."

After dinner, they retired to Lord Smith's chambers. From the window she could see the gardens extending far off into the horizon, a maze of geometric patterns and colors that dazzled in the daylight but sort of loomed in the night. Lord Smith stood behind her and brushed the straps from her shoulders, and she wriggled her body so that the dress fell to the floor.

He kissed her neck again, and she leaned back, letting her head rest on his chest. He turned her around and looked her up and down. She pushed him backwards, and led him to the edge of the bed where he sat down, and she brought him to her breasts.

She hoped he wouldn't notice the scars. The plastic surgeon had made the incisions in the nook where her breast met her torso, and in the dim light it must nearly blend in, but still she worried. He grabbed each breast and lifted them, rubbing his fingers over her areola. She moaned and he leaned forward to place his lips over her left nipple.

She brought her hands to her chest and squeezed under her breast on the little silicon cartridge, ejecting a single dose of poison into his mouth. Immediately he sputtered and choked, and pushed her away from him, and put his hands around his throat. The poison swelled his tongue and tonsils, and within moments the sputtering became a choked hum as the airway completely sealed. She stood over him, naked, alone, and wondered if she'd ever leave this compound again.

37

POSTER BOY

ENDLESSBONERZ

National State-Mandated GF Day was all Werther had been able to think about since getting his invitation in the mail. The tradition dated back to 2025, when President Trump vowed to grant the wishes of his most loyal followers. One young man asked for an "art hoe who can't say no." And so, a national holiday was born. Now, once a year, a select few who provided an "invaluable service" to the expansion of the One True American Empire are granted the opportunity to pick their forever girlfriend.

Werther's day had finally come. As he strode down the halls of the Winter White House to the chamber where Barron Trump was holding court, Werther pictured himself slobbering on a beautiful breast no bigger than a mouthful. His burgeoning erection was interrupted by Barron's security flinging open the doors leading to the Emperor himself.

Werther bowed.

"Welcome, welcome young Werther. Your posting exploits have been an inspiration." Barron had come to the throne after his father's ten-year reign, and despite numerous successes at home and abroad, internet posting was just as important now as it was then. While the communists were on their heels, it was vital to keep the mockery going as it made doing the dirty work more palatable to the masses. Short memories can let pity creep back into the hearts of those who would unwittingly allow the deformed within the gates again.

"I am honored to be here, Your Highness."

Barron smiled. "So tell me, what kind of forever girlfriend do you wish to have? Tall? Short? Petite? Muscular? Young and virginal? Or perhaps something a little more experienced?"

Bowing again, Werther asked Emperor Trump if he had seen Neon Genesis Evangelion. Grinning now, Barron mused, "I see we have a Rei versus Asuka question on our hands."

Werther blushed. "Misato Katsuragi."

A massive mainframe, previously unnoticed by Werther, lit up and began to whirl behind Barron Trump. The room was silent except for the fans dutifully keeping the mainframe cool. At last, the whirl died down and a voice, one oddly familiar to Werther, permeated the room: "A match has been identified."

Barron caught the recognition in Werther's eyes. "A familiar voice?"

"That's Rudy Giuliani's voice, isn't it?"

"My dad had a soft spot for that old lecherous perv, so I thought it would be fun to use his voice for the forever girlfriend hunts. Do you like?"

"'Your tits are mine,'" said Werther in his best Giuliani imitation. Barron howled with laughter and Werther caught a few of his security guards grinning.

When Barron regained his composure, he commanded, "RudyBot, tell Werther about his forever girlfriend."

"Emily Rosenblatt, single mother of three boys. Two of her boys were fathered by Tyrone, and the other boy was fathered by a Marquise DeKwan. Emily works in journalism and is thirty-four years old. She also..." Werther stopped listening. All the posting. All the memes. All of it led to him being shackled to a single mom who was...

"Damnit RudyBot, if you could see the look on Werther's face you would know that it is not funny!" Werther snapped out of it and looked at Barron, who despite his stern tone, clearly found RudyBot's teasing highly amusing. "I'm sorry about that. No matter how many times I tell him not to, he still does it. RudyBot, tell him..."

"Emily Winter is five foot ten, weighs 104 pounds, and is nineteen years old. She has a 120 IQ, perky A-cups, and a personality match of over eighty percent to one fictional anime character, Misato Katsuragi."

Werther bowed and placed his hands in front of him to hide the growth in his pants. "Thank you, RudyBot," he stuttered. "And thank you, Your Highness."

"You can thank me by continuing to post. Don't let that tight piece of trim slow you down. We still need you, you hear?"

"Yes, sir!"

"NEXT!" shouted Barron as Werther was escorted from the room.

38

VAMPIRE ISLAND

BRONZE AGE PERVERT

There is a tropical smell like fresh cut grass, moist earth, musty sea mosses, you can taste sometimes in silver type of high powered cane juice rum, real rum; it breathes in you warmth and mist where you descend into a kind of bosom haze. This feeling was the dearest possession of the men of LC battalion, short for "Lewis and Clark." The majestic sight of the gulf with volcanic rock hills jutting out of vegetation, the ocean, the trees and lush dark green foliage by the beach, their encampment in the clearing—it had long ago stopped being a modern military-style camp with perimeter and guards and was now a free community with men putting up their individual hovels where it pleased them; much as Tacitus describes the ancient Germanic—these sights and easy life was their pleasure. And for some of the more sensitive, above all the refreshing fragrant smell of grasses and herbs and running streams every morning was a pleasure. Very few had bothered to remember exactly how they got here. Some years ago after nuclear war that flattened cities they had been sent to secure Guam, but they found nothing when they got there. Communications with the mainland were then suddenly cut off again. They had two working vessels and they had moved far across the ocean, island to island, until they found this one, which was comfortable. Hardly anything needed to be done to secure food or fresh water, and in an abandoned depot they found silos full of petrol. In idyllic tropics comfort, many liked to forget.

The men of LC battalion had preserved two features of their otherwise forgotten military life. One was physical fitness; along with hygiene this was a necessity on a tropical island where they still had to move frequently and fast, on hunts and fishing and such where excess flesh was an obstacle, besides being often mocked... it was not possible to hide—the humid air meant clothmos weren't comfortable. There was also a bust of the Blond Beast, featured at center of their former camp, framed with majestic palm fronds; this had been displayed in the commander's quarters on ship. The figure of The Lion, the president and redeemer of the former nation, was now revered almost as idol even by those of the soldiers who preserved their old religion. As for the commander himself, he had no further authority in this situation, but was respected as first among equals and often addressed with the friendly honorific "subcomandante," maybe tongue-in-cheek. Otherwise, the comrades of LC had grown so comfortable and in such lovely languor that they hadn't even bothered to explore fully the interior of the island. They shared joke stories about what may be in the forests leading up to central volcano, and small groups planned to visit it "really soon."

It is from the dark forest on the mountain that their doom came down. Two, then three men disappeared on night walks, fishing trips and reveries, and in battalion of 500 this was soon felt—when five more disappeared and had not come back for two weeks, it was no longer likely friends had just left on usual personal outings. *Something is taking us.* It was also noticed over the following weeks that the most conspicuously handsome and fit men were being picked off. Immediately military instincts reasserted—*they are taking us apart piecemeal, starting with the strongest.* In response to this danger, Subcomandante Carlssen was granted full title again and chain of command was reestablished. The men regrouped in tents in the camp, guarded at night, and an expeditionary armed force of 100 of those most skilled in forest was tasked with penetrating deep jungle that began at volcano foothills.

Commander Carlssen lost contact with two platoons—dazed, in deep terror the remaining thirty-three men under his direct command made way up thick mountain paths... until they saw. The cause of terror... in horror but also excitement they saw, from behind dense monstera on a ridge: sophisticated structures, town on stilts. In center marketplace there was a gathering: their lost comrades were fully nude and pumping into writhing, moaning women on banana-leaf "rugs." Around them were gathered many women, fully nude but also fully armed, some with headbands, some with skulls around waist, applauding and cheering the lewd proceedings. They watched in fascination their comrades' rippling muscles, sweat dripping down in sunset light as they undulated pumping relentlessly into the frenzied gripping pussies of the ecstatic amazons. Some of the excited onlookers occasionally lashed the soldiers obviously used as breeding studs. In shock they saw also their recently captured comrades, entirely nude, menaced by sharp arrows and AK-47s, as other amazon-maidens were hosing them down with cold spring water, cleaning them. While on others they were applying various perfumes and oils, preparing them surely for hours of exhausting copulation.

Incapacitated by both shock and lust, Carlssen's platoon hesitated, then decided to return to camp. The amazons numbered in the thousands—3,000 lithe, savage, well-armed and trained... violent vampiric cum huntresses. After debate, LC battalion, torn apart by conflicting feelings, some men wishing for surrender, nevertheless attempted a rescue operation. Face to face in lush jungle valley at foot of mountains, the opposing armies, almost locked in struggle, came to agreement: out of true struggle great Constitutions are born. The men of LC battalion surrendered and graciously agreed to be used as breeding studs so that the race may continue, but gave conditions: no more than three extractions per day, and this only a week at a time, with days of rest in between, fed shellfish, pineapple, and cured wild boar by the amazons' dwarflike servant class. A Constitution based on the American Anti-Federalist papers of 1787-8 was ratified, and a New America was founded in South Pacific. The men soon found that amazons' lust for cum and fucking knew no bounds, however, and was not constrained by merely reproductive justifications.

39

GROWING PAINS

T. PORTRA

Mom and Dad stopped loving each other some time ago. For my sake, they stuck it out, but I could tell that the marriage was doomed. We all could. I waited for the collapse, but instead, Mom and Dad came to me one afternoon and sat me down, and told me they had a plan that would save their marriage and keep the family together.

"Brian," Mom said, "things are going to change."

"For the better," Dad added.

Mom knelt in front of me so that it was hard not to look her in the eye.

"Your Dad and I have been accepted into New York's Parental Gender Reassignment Program. Your Dad and I are going to trade places. I'm going to be Dad."

"And I'm going to be Mom," Dad said. "How's that sound?"

It took two weeks for Mom and Dad to recover after their surgeries. At first, I was skeptical, but I have to say, after the bandages came off, I was even more skeptical. Either the surgeons' work was flawless—ten years of sentience was long enough to understand that no one, not even a professional, was that good—or else Mom and Dad were playing a prank on me because I didn't notice any sign of change. *Mom* looked like Mom had looked before, and *Dad* looked like, well, he looked like Dad. Soon I convinced myself that my parents were playing a joke and I was its butt.

Over the coming week, I kept my distance and observed. *Mom* and *Dad* seemed to sense my anxiety and didn't push the issue.

Like a cop, I scrutinized their behavior, looking for discrepancies and subtle violations of the natural order. If my parents had swapped places, surely they'd have carried over longstanding habits and various other unshakable peccadillos.

For instance, formerly, whenever Dad had performed a menial task—shaving, cooking, weeding, or whatever—he would hum to himself in this specific-absent-drone-like way, almost like a buzzing bee. So when *Mom* swept, I trailed *her*, listening. Later, when *she* ironed the tablecloth in our kitchen, I listened some more. But I heard no humming, nothing reminiscent of a buzzing bee.

Next, I manufactured a scenario that was bound to prove my hypothesis. I unscrewed the legs on my play chairs and brought the pieces to *Dad*. Dad could easily fix a few chairs, no problem, but when it came to handy work, Mom had been as useless as tits on a keyboard. *Dad* placed the pieces on the floor and then left the room. I'd be lying if I said I didn't feel smug. But my self-satisfaction faded when *Dad* returned with a screwdriver and quickly set to putting my play chairs back together.

Rattled but undeterred, I sought council and asked our AI, House Helper™, what the difference between a man and a woman was. She spoke words that I didn't understand. So I asked her for a picture, and on my wall, she displayed a diagram of the male and female anatomy side by side. After scrutinizing the diagram, I concluded that the key to proving my hypothesis was with the genitals.

The next day—it was a sunny Saturday—*Mom* and *Dad* were drinking martinis by the pool. I waited until their glasses looked empty and then offered to make them fresh drinks. I faked a big dumb grin—they loved that stuff. *Mom* and *Dad* seemed happy that I seemed happy, and they gave me their empty glasses and I went into the house and up to Mom and Dad's bedroom, opened the medicine cabinet, and got a couple Klonopins and some Ambien. I swallowed a Klonopin. I figured I better battle my anxiety before it took root. I wanted to appear collected when I brought *Mom* and *Dad* their cocktails. In the kitchen, I crushed up the Ambiens and the

Klonopins and I sprinkled all if it into two gin-heavy martinis. I threw in extra olives to mask the metallic taste of the drugs. I figured it couldn't hurt to be careful.

"Wow!" I said, handing *Mom her* martini, "what a beautiful afternoon."

"It is lovely, isn't it," *she* agreed.

I tried to recall if lovely was a word Dad had regularly used.

"Lovely," *Dad* agreed, accepting *his* martini.

I went inside and upstairs to my bedroom. To pass the time I masturbated three or four times, stopping only after my dick was too raw to continue self-flagellating.

I went outside. The sun had dipped behind the pool house. *Mom* and *Dad* were unconscious. *Mom* was half out of *her* chaise lounge, only *her* lower half was still seated, making it easy to inspect *her* vagina.

I moved *Mom's* bikini bottom to one side. The vagina was a mix of wrinkles and folds. I inspected *Dad's* penis but there was nothing about it that offered me relief.

Back inside I sulked on the couch. I tried to watch tv but couldn't follow anything. I asked House Helper™ if Parental Reassignment was a real thing.

"Hmm," House Helper™ mused (an affection I loathed), "let me check, Brian."

I rolled my eyes.

"According to my search, Parental Reassignment was developed in the People's Republic of China by..."

House Helper™ continued on, but I stopped listening. My attention was toward the sliding glass door which had just opened. My parents were standing in the living room. Both were completely naked.

Dad said, "Brian, call an ambulance. Your *mom* and *dad* are very ill."

40

OKEECHOBEE CARPET DELIVERY SERVICE

FAISAL MARZIPAN

Blake Pfluger had counted the steps—sixteen to the second floor and ten to the loft—noted the 2020 French door Wolf refrigerator and the Aga oven. He had lightly touched Jared's arm and said, "They must have been professional chefs."

When Blake first met the Hoffmans, he pitched house hunting as a kind of a date. Intimate discussions about the kind of school district their future kids may enroll in, the pros and mostly cons of modern stucco. Backlit address plates. The entirety of the Lake Eola aesthetic. All while Blake chauffeured them in his burnt orange Land Rover Defender.

"So the beauty of this townhome is—in this neighborhood—is first-floor living. That's pretty rare. And it's less than twenty years old." Blake locked eyes with Jared, acknowledging that it was he and not Chelsea who would be the key decision maker.

"It's been on the market for five days. I can tell you, it won't be on the market for long. What do you think?"

Jared shuffled nervously. "It just seems like seven-fifty is a little overpriced for a townhome."

Blake shrugged. "Well, that's because it's a corner property. And a 2005 build is pretty recent for Lake Eola."

"The one on Amelia was seven-eighty," Chelsea said with a mousy twitch. "And that was on the market only three days. They say you should budget about thirty to forty percent of your combined salary. Between the law firm and the hospital, you think you could pull it off?"

You wouldn't be able to tell Blake used eyeliner unless you got within about three feet. He kept the bronzer to a bare minimum as well. Blake's mom took him to see Pinocchio for making all As in third grade, and for the rest of his childhood he dreamed of working at Disney World. His first summer after college, he interned at Disney and after rolling around with the boys at Buena Vista Lay for a year, the very concept of sitting in a classroom and biding his time seemed pointless. His career trajectory ran from Disney to waiting table to HIV counseling to realty, and now Blake Pfluger's name can be found on as many Orlando signs as there are twinks at the Republican National Convention (and Blake would know). These bored housewives that made up most of the realty business couldn't keep up with him.

Of course, the Hoffmans agreed to buy. Now it was just time to line up his finance guy. Behind the pristine, youthful face of Blake was a veritable cottage industry. His finance guy, the title company, structural engineers, cleaning crews, inspectors, renovators, exterminators, landscaping. Blake could name two people to do each job. After pre-approval, Blake dropped the Hoffmans off at their apartment and finally checked his phone while at a stoplight. Julio, his contractor, texted him that Jackrabbit Joe was squatting in a townhome while it was being built. Jackrabbit Joe was well known on neighborhood watch apps for his quick grab-and-go thefts—bikes and tools out of people's garages. Most of the vagrants and squatters stayed west of I-4.

Sitting at the stoplight, Blake Pfluger narrowed his eyes and said, "Not Lake Eola."

Blake called Julio.

"Yes Mister Blake."

"What's going on?"

"We are still working the plumbing. You know I drop my helper off Mister Blake. I forgot my toolbox at the house and when I come this Jackrabbit, he staying there. I can see him in the window."

"Hold on, do you think he's armed?"

"I don't know Mister Blake."

"Ok, I'm coming."

Blake had started taking CrossFit seriously in his mid-thirties. He could network, and it gave him a chance to stay in the sauna. Sometimes he would let his rent boys have a guest pass to Club Orlando. Blake also started taking jiu-jitsu, mostly to practice rolling around with Disney interns while on poppers and Cialis on a weekend binge. But, Blake knew, he needed to know these skills.

Blake met Julio.

"Did he leave yet?"

"No Mister Blake."

"We're going to scare him off."

"Ok."

Blake motioned Julio to follow him. The front door had a resettable code lock. Jackrabbit must have broken a double-paned Renewal by Andersen window to squat. Three-hundred to replace.

"Do you have a gun?"

"No Mister Blake, not here."

"Ok, well, just act like you do. We need to scare him out of Lake Eola. Ready?"

Julio threw back his shoulders on his 5'2 frame. "Yes Mister Blake."

Blake Pfluger silently counted to three with his fingers and quickly opened the hardwood door.

"OK JACKRABBIT GET OUT, GET OUT OF HERE."

Jackrabbit Joe's eyes widened and he bolted for the garage, but as was his nature, grabbed Julio's toolbox on the way out.

"CUCARACHA!" Julio yelled and met Jackrabbit Joe in the foyer. Jackrabbit was the bigger man, but Julio relentlessly wrenched the toolbox from his grip, scattering tools on the marble tile floor. Jackrabbit put his hands around Julio's neck, which Blake noted was not an effective choke. Still, Julio was struggling, and looked to Blake.

Blake picked up a monkey wrench and instinctively slammed it down on Jackrabbit Joe's head.

"AAAARRGH. YOU HIT ME. YOU HIT ME. MUFUGGGGAAAH," hollered Jackrabbit, holding his hands to his bloody head.

At this point, Julio looked at Blake and in a single gesture signaled as co-conspirator and colleague, as if to say, "Well Mister Blake, let's finish the job."

Blake landed the monkey wrench again and again on the back of Jackrabbit Joe's head until he was silent. Blake's erection was massive, no Cialis necessary. He locked the door, and panting, sat on the foyer stairs.

"Wat we gon do now Mr. Blake?"

"Now we finish the job. Do we have any leftover carpet?"

"Sure Mister Blake."

"Let's wrap him up."

"And then wat."

"Then we dispose of the body, Julio. Tell Concepcion you are working late tonight. Look, I am in the top three percent of realtors in Orlando. And I'd like to keep it that way. And, Julio, I'm quite sure you don't feel like going back to Venezuela. Am I right?"

"No Mister Blake."

"Ok, so here's the plan," Blake said, making strong eye contact. "We roll Jackrabbit in the carpet and load him into your van."

"My van?"

"I can't put him in the Defender. Then, together, we go to Okeechobee."

"Why so far?"

"That's where they burn the sugar cane. You didn't think we were going to feed the alligators, did you?"

Thankfully, the carpet was cheap and Jackrabbit Joe fit perfectly. Julio backed his van into the garage and together they loaded the carpet into the back. Blake sneered at the Taco Bell wrappers on the passenger seat.

"You know, you should get Concepcion to clean this."

"Ok Mister Blake."

41

THE RED DESERT FATHERS

THE NEXT MAZER

The settlement ship descended into the valley beneath the dome of a dormant volcano, scattering its cloud of red dust a safe distance from the station. The fathers emerged, clad in simple white survival suits, and walked in wordless single file down the rocky path to Echelon base.

It was a fitting place for banishment: A cluster of indistinguishable gray boxes, dropped at the earliest convenience onto the floor of a valley the color of bone. Unlike the abbey Earth's bureaucrats had stripped from them, this terraforming outpost had never heard the sound of birdsong, or been repaired by a human hand. A joke had spread among the bureaucrats that the peace and quiet might do the fathers some good.

Ahead, two gold suits flashed in the thin sunlight. Echelon's scientists waited for them.

Terse conversations followed in rooms filled with resentment. The fathers understood. Echelon's destiny as the first step towards a world grown without nations or borders had crashed on the hard rocks of economic viability. So they sat, and listened, and gracefully accepted stewardship of the station's data stores and security codes.

The fathers didn't watch as the scientists' ship traced an arc of fire over the volcano's dome. It no longer belonged to their world. They gathered to pray, and bestow a new name upon their home. Life in Exile had begun.

Mars lived up to its namesake. Each day the war god's demons of dust cackled and clawed at Exile's walls, mocking the fathers' effort to survive in the valley. Nights brought their own torments—grinning specters of death that emerged from behind the veil of dreams. But monastic life's rigors had accustomed the fathers to spiritual warfare. They clung to their rule, praying to their god and working the barren land.

Slowly, the isolation that had driven Echelon's scientists to the edge of sanity became a haven for the monastics of Exile. Ancient rituals took on the shape of their new calendar. The Martian solar year, twice the length of Earth's, was embroidered with the feasts of forgotten saints and lost seasons.

Above all, there was silence. Surrounded by the planet's arid calm, the fathers found silence truer, and deeper, than any imaginable back home. This absolute stillness, coupled with long fasts intensified by the rationing of the foodstores, allowed the fathers to experience visions and raptures of the divine.

Their faith belonged to the desert once again.

A second ship landed in the shadow of the volcano. Another monastery's lands had been taken, its occupants sent to Exile. Earth's bureaucrats expected resistance, but received none. In the eyes of the fathers, strong hands sent from above could be nothing if not a gift from God. They thanked the pilots and blessed them—a gesture that haunted their long trip home.

Terraforming now began in earnest, with a forthrightness born of the stakes of survival. The fathers anthilled the volcano, working to create a network of farming tunnels splashed with UV light and warmed by the heart of the planet. Mars did not yield easily. Several tunnels collapsed early on, consuming weeks of toil. The fathers discovered Exile's seismic monitoring equipment failed to differentiate their movements within the tunnels from that of the mountain itself.

In response, they simply disabled the monitoring instruments and improved their excavation methods. Much was left to God.

A third ship came, putting the base well over its official capacity, but the fathers opened their doors without complaint. Later, it would be discovered they had retrofitted the station's laboratories into living quarters. Idle questions no longer served Exile's purpose.

Remarkably, the first harvest came in ahead of schedule. They had broken the spine of the war god. The valley was theirs.

When the fourth ship's door opened, its pilots looked out in astonishment. One of the fathers stood there with smiling eyes, his face covered by nothing except a ragged cloth to cut the Martian chill. The terraforming machines had thickened the valley's atmosphere enough to breathe, at least for lungs adjusted to the thin air.

The father offered hospitality, which they accepted. They donned respirators and followed him, awestruck, through the valley of Exile. Silver streams of water cracked the ground, feeding low, hardy plants whose green hue was not so different from the greens of earth. That evening, the fathers served their visitors a simple meal of vegetables and protein in the farming tunnels. From somewhere deep in the volcano came the chanting of psalms. The stone rang with ancient language.

When the pilots returned and spoke of their experiences, they were careful to avoid using the word "miraculous." But those on Earth who believed in secret heard the truth, and began to seek passage to the garden in the desert.

The Martian oasis grew steadily, as more and more of the hidden faithful came to settle the valley. The fathers withdrew to a ring of shelters fringing the habitable zone, so they could remain in the desert's silence and surround the faithful with their prayers.

And all the while, from across the gulf of space, the bureaucrats watched with envious eyes.

Defying all official predictions, the once-failed settlement had become valuable again. Various interest groups now vied to take their place in history as the first true founders of a new planet. The bureaucrats would sort out the details, but it quickly became clear what this would mean for the meddlesome religious sect.

Exile's time had come to an end.

The fathers boarded another settlement vessel, more powerful than the one that brought them to Mars generations earlier. They didn't look down as the desert sank from view and the pilots took them to a new outpost built atop the subterranean oceans of Europa.

A joke spread among the bureaucrats as they tracked the ship's journey deep into the solar system. Maybe, they said, if the fathers traveled far enough into the darkness of space, they would find their God there waiting for them.

42

BROKEN ARROW

MARTY PHILLIPS

"Captain Wilson, please remain calm. The waking process has been initiated. Verify mission passphrase when you are ready."

He submerged in the dream again after the moment of fleeting awareness.

"Atypical landing detected. Life support stable. Earthbound communication stable. Sensor systems not communicating. Internal computer has sustained data loss and is running limited operation functionality."

Then, with a renewed awareness, he remembered the Arbalest Program.

"Captain, once you have recovered fully from deep sleep process, please establish communication with headquarters and verify status."

He had landed. What was it called again? Object K-731. Once his fingers could move, he activated the wake stim injector and winced as a flood of tingling warmth and mental clarity coursed through him. Daniel flopped out of the sleep chamber and onto the floor of the Argus-1 command module. Once his legs found enough strength, he staggered into the research module and found the bank of monitors dead.

"What's this about the internal computer?" he slurred over his thick tongue after dragging himself up into the chair.

"Research module computer failure. Sensor control offline. Probe control offline."

"Call command. This is Captain Daniel Wilson confirming mission code: archer libra eschaton."

"Confirmed, establishing connection."

It took nearly twenty minutes for the call to connect. Daniel was just beginning to worry that one of the repeaters dropped by the craft on its journey may have failed, when a familiar voice spoke to him over the vastness of space.

"Danny, are you there?"

He smiled. "Ollie, yes. It's me. Argus-1 has landed."

"It's damned good to hear you. Can you see me on the monitor?"

"No, things got a little banged up on the landing. I'll need help remotely. My monitors are dead."

"Let me log into the system and see what I can find."

"Is Alex there, and Jerry and the rest of the team?"

"No, it's just me today."

The captain felt an ominous twinge. "Am I off schedule? I know I'm not the center of the universe, but I was expecting a little more celebration."

Oliver Nelson let out a quick bark of a laugh. It had always been a tell for his discomfort. "Ten years is a long time, Danny. The rest of us didn't get to spend it sleeping. I was able to pull data remotely. Some of it is corrupted."

"What can I do in the meantime?"

"Proceed with what you can on the mission agenda. I'll call you back soon."

The call ended abruptly.

Something was wrong. Daniel returned to the command module and completed the health diagnostic before moving to the window and staring out into a dense, swirling fog. He hoped that the damage to the craft would not prevent him from walking the surface. He received a call back nearly six hours later.

"Hello, Danny? It's Ollie. I'm trying to salvage what information I can, but it's slow going."

"Why not send it up to Peters in Mission Data?"

"Peters isn't with the program anymore."

"Ok, then send it to his replacement."

The other man sighed. "It's not a matter of who replaced him. It's structural. Politics, you know?"

The captain's frustration boiled over. "No. I don't know. You're being evasive."

"It's not appropriate for me to discuss. Hang in there, buddy. I'll call back."

Daniel spent the next eight hours taking apart the research module computer and determining if any part of the failure was accessible from the inside of the ship. Then he deployed the sleeping hammock on the anchors inside the hull and finally slept. The buzzing of the comms system woke him.

"Ollie, please tell me you have good news."

The voice that replied was unfamiliar and belonged to a woman.

"Hello, am I speaking to Captain Daniel Wilson?"

"Yes, who is this?"

"This is program director Sandra Ramirez."

"What happened to Thomas Drygaslki?"

"He is no longer with the Arbalest Program."

Daniel's heart sank. "Please excuse my curtness, but I've been asleep for ten years, and now I'm all alone countless miles from home on a ship that's damaged, and I've only been able to speak to one engineer, and nobody I know seems to work with the program anymore. I'm beginning to get rather concerned."

"I'm willing to answer your questions."

"Why is nobody there anymore?"

"Because the program was effectively ended."

"What? Arbalest was the most ambitious space project in history!"

"Yes, and the last thing we want to do is give credit to the former regime."

"But this accomplishment belongs to all Americans, regardless of politics."

Ramirez let out a mocking laugh. "You are such an artifact of the past. What does your little space venture mean for the immigrant farm laborer, or the black boy from the inner city who never got a shot at a good life?"

"I don't understand."

“Of course you don’t. Your kind never did. Even ten years ago, you should have seen the seeds. The Party did not come out of nowhere.”

“So, then what about me? Am I just stuck out here?”

“We aren’t heartless. We’re bringing in a few of our people to try to get you back quietly, but all other mission considerations are cancelled. What’s most important is the story. You failed, and we saved you. I’ll give you time to process, captain.”

Despair washed over him, but sudden resolve followed. Daniel crossed to the airlock and donned his spacesuit before activating the door.

“Warning. Sensor failure. Cannot establish surface conditions. Do not depart the craft.”

“Override,” he stated firmly.

He entered the chamber and opened the far door. His boots touched the planet’s rocky surface. Daniel clambered uphill through the fog to a rise that overlooked a valley where the air was clear and green vegetation swayed in the breeze. Then he removed the helmet and felt the warmth of the pale blue sun on his face. His lungs drew in the air. He could not be sure what all had happened back on Earth during his sleep, but he had no desire to return as a pawn for some new politics. He alone would carry on the dream, holding it cradled within like a secret fire.

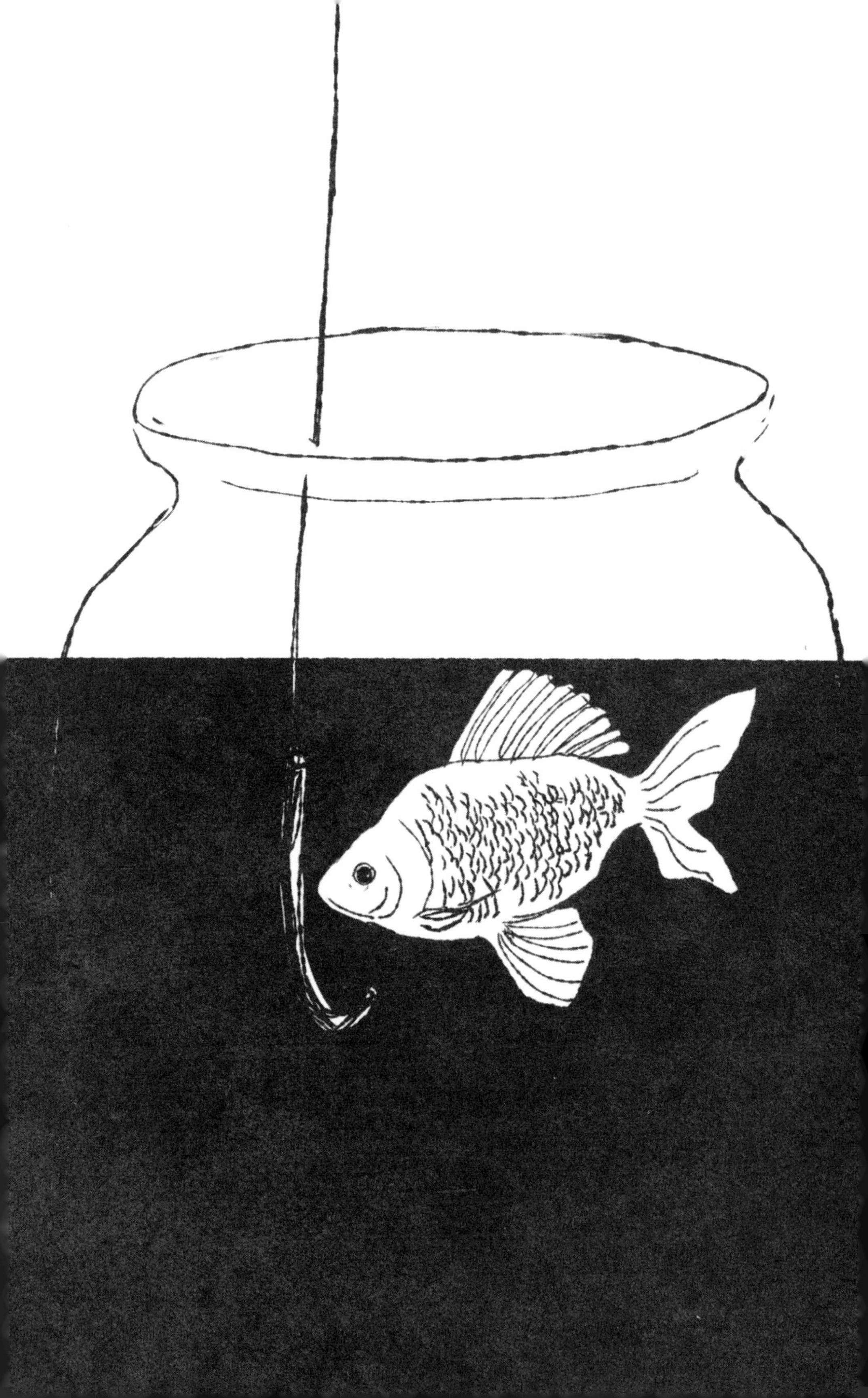

43

FISHING ON MARS

T.R. HUDSON

I despise the artificial. My stomach has never settled with lab-grown meat, instead rejecting it and punishing me for subjecting it to the horrors of the frankenburger.

When they claimed to terraform Mars, I dreamt it was another Eden, but alas I arrived to a collection of snow globes with central air and army cots. Ishmael and I prefer the water. In space, there is no great leviathan ready to swallow you whole and no Poseidon to appease with gifts and prayers and promises to be more than we are. There is no god of space. Can there be a god of nothing?

Ishmael swims in his bowl and though he can't see it, he knows he is confined, forever encased in his snow globe, watching the unexplainable without even the comfort of another to attest to his sanity. Were I a more powerful and merciful god, I would flood the craters of Mars and give Ishmael dominion over it and supply him a harem of appealing mates. Instead, he must make do as steward of the artificial plants and plastic castle and praise my name when the bits of fish food sink down to him from outside his firmament.

I've tried to walk the rusted iron dust of the war god, but even then, I find no freedom there, just a smaller globe for me to dance in like the hula girls of Maui.

I wonder if Mister Musk felt cheated when he first stepped out of the craft. He was old by then, much older than he'd hoped to be. A whole lifetime on Earth just to bring home a rock and die hitting on his nurse. But who am I to judge? No one, and I prefer it that way.

The coxswain is heard yet unnoticed among the strapping rowers. His job could be done by a drum machine and a couple forty-five-pound plates. So too, I wish the role of crazy old man could have been filled by a mannequin or wax figure. Let him be the scapegoat for my children's problems. Let him be rocketed to an old folks' home on Mars. When he dies, he can be cremated and create the first Martian soil to sustain life. I just wanted my cabin and rod.

Social time is asocial. They put us in a giant snowglobe and put on music that was dated and old when we were young. Haven't seen any women yet. My wife passed some years before and I did not re-marry. It's been so long that I often wonder if my rod and tackle even still work. Maybe they put the women on Venus.

Today was an auspicious day. Ishmael and I, being bosom chums of great stature along the lines of those Myrmidonen heroes, have decided together to bring sport into our lives. Me, his hunter and he, my prey. I found some dental floss and a bit of tin foil, which I fashioned into a rudimentary fish hook. Better men have won more with less.

Ishmael is a great adversary. Cunning, stoic and void of vindictiveness. Were I Jonah, it would be some other, less fish who'd get me, not my noble friend. We battled until dinner. Sitting that long hurts my knees and I imagine that Ishmael could use the break to recover as well.

A few weeks into our duel, he bit on a chunk of fake meat that I smuggled from the cafeteria. Hook, line, sinker and I hoisted Ishmael out of the water. Then, with the gentle care of a father to a newborn, I relaxed him back into the bowl. They say goldfish have no memory. A pity. I'll remember this victory for the rest of my life.

Ishmael has diminished as of late. His shrewd mind has become careless and catching him has lost its edge. Maybe it's man's curse. After a while, a master no longer faces adversity. I make a decision then and there: we will go to Neptune. A place like that must have a lot of water and maybe a few fish worthy of my skill. Ishmael agrees—we will steal a rocket tomorrow.

I go down to sleep and notice how round my belly has gotten. Damn frankenburgers. I'll be having real food soon enough. I look over at my pal and see he's already left without me, asleep on his back, too. He's small and will need the head start. As if I wouldn't carry him with me. That old so and so. I don't know much about rockets, but we'll figure it out. Two keen minds such as ours can devise this techno-babble. They'll bang on my door and wonder where I've left to and I'll just have a crude sign on the wall. Gone Fishin'.

44

THE ARC OF THE MORAL UNIVERSE SLOUCHES TOWARDS BETHLEHEM

JUSTIN LEE

One day, we—that is, the world, all of us—got sick of racism. We also got sick of sexism, ageism, ableism, ethnocentrism, heterosexism, the whole shebang of -isms, -normativities, and -phobias. People were different from one another and that caused a lot of problems. So it all had to go. Difference, that is. Difference had to go.

We settled on the obvious course of action: eugenics. It wasn't all that difficult. Everyone already lived everywhere. Things were pretty well mixed up. We just mixed them up even more. We bred difference out of the species.

Well, most of it. There were still biological males and biological females, but you couldn't tell by looking at them. We bred the men smaller and the women bigger until everyone equaled out to a healthy 5'8" and 140 lbs., give or take. We embarked on a rigorous course of intermarriage, mixing and remixing until we reduced the cursed human palette to a gentle monochrome. An insensitive bigot of a few centuries ago might have called us "vaguely ethnic." We all tan pretty well in summer and get a little ashy in winter. We have the most lovely hazel eyes.

Our women have narrower hips than they once did and their breasts are the same size as our men's. We did away with body and facial hair and rounded our chins and narrowed our shoulders and equalized our intelligence. We bred our clitorises larger and our penises smaller until one was as good as the other. We all have thick auburn hair and no cancer.

Religion was a pain in our collective ass for a long time. So we bred for increased connectivity in our right parietal lobes. Cathedrals and mosques and temples fell into disrepair and their stones were repurposed. No one seemed to mind.

Property was the next to go. What need did we have for money and marriage?

Once we were finally equal and not a single difference remained—save for the occasional blonde or unusually thick hair, which was promptly tweezed—we cured aging and sterilized ourselves. We became beautiful, bipedal mules. Sex was now consequence-free, though few still found it that interesting.

Racial epithets became meaningless, for there were no more races. No one spoke an unkind word to anyone else, not even for the sake of humor. Humor is impossible without difference.

We were all brothers and sisters. History had ended in a new Eden. Finally, there was perfect peace on earth.

Until there wasn't.

We grew bored. Every moment was the same as every other. Time had no meaning. The cycle of day and night became tedious, insulting. Existence throbbed with mundanity. We longed for the heat death of the universe.

In our eagerness to become brothers and sisters, we had forgotten that siblings quarrel.

We saw ourselves and only ourselves in every face we encountered. Unable to endure the violence of that sameness, we fought. We threw ourselves against one another like protons in a sealed container. We killed and mutilated indiscriminately, for there was no basis upon which to discriminate.

At first we rejoiced in the slaughter. Rendering our enemies corpses made them different than us. Our identity was aliveness, an identity sustainable only by negating the aliveness of others. And so we negated with savage delight, determining ourselves as ourselves again and again.

But as our numbers dwindled we began to see that such self-determination had only made us more like our fellows. The horror was unbearable.

None of us remember who first proposed the solution. All we know is that a wary truce was followed by a pillaging of the long-neglected institutions of memory. We scoured the libraries and museums for legacies of forgotten difference. We relearned the old languages, which were all so different from our Universal Pidgin. It was difficult, but we reveled in that difficulty. Soon we pronounced the names of dead gods and chanted the rituals once used to worship them. We learned the rhythms of the Zuni rain dance and the sacred words spoken over dead Norsemen as their pyres were lit and their gray spirits unfurled toward Valhalla. We discovered that Atman is Brahman and memorized the Apostles' Creed. We dressed ourselves in the vestments of a thousand faiths and carved our flesh with the insignia of Mesopotamian deities. We became Vestal Virgins and Mongolian shamans, Maasai warriors and peace-loving Jains. We sacrificed to Baal and then tore down his altar in the name of the Prophet, peace be upon him. We pantomimed the old animosities and were relieved.

With exquisite care we distributed genuine artifacts of difference, pearls of memory, and took up the mantels of forgotten peoples. We danced in the streets, relishing our imagined otherness, a people of constant carnival.

Some day, we know, the disguise will lose its power. In our darker moments we feel the swell of sameness beneath our masks. The pageantry of appropriations will soon run to riot. Crisis looms. Perhaps it will be our last. But until then—we dance.